"You said the babe is not yours?"

Raesha Bawell's pretty face paled to a porcelain white. "We found her on our porch night before last," she said, her gray eyes stormy with emotion.

Josiah's heart beat too fast. He took in a breath. "Found her?"

"*Ja*. Someone left her in a basket with a few supplies and a note."

"Her bonnet," he said. "Could I take a look at it?"

Raesha lifted the dainty little knit cap from the baby's head and handed it over to Josiah. He clutched the soft, warm fabric, his eyes misting when he saw what he'd been looking for. "There," he said. "My *mamm* stitched my sister's initials in the tiny cap. DJF. Deidre Josephine Fisher. Josie loved that little hat. She took it with her when she left."

Josie's sudden departure from Kentucky had rattled Josiah to the core. Now he felt hopeful for the first time in the last year of searching for his sister. Josie could still be nearby.

He hated to hurt Raesha any further, but he had to believe what his eyes were telling him. "*Ja*, I do think this *bobbeli* could be my sister's baby."

With over seventy books published and millions in print, **Lenora Worth** writes award-winning romance and romantic suspense. Three of her books were finalists in the ACFW Carol Awards, and her Love Inspired Suspense novel *Body of Evidence* became a *New York Times* bestseller. Her novella in *Mistletoe Kisses* made her a *USA TODAY* bestselling author. Lenora goes on adventures with her retired husband, Don, and enjoys reading, baking and shopping…especially shoe shopping.

Visit the Author Profile page at Harlequin.com for more titles.

Her Amish Child

Lenora Worth

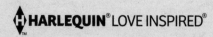
HARLEQUIN® LOVE INSPIRED®

Recycling programs
for this product may
not exist in your area.

LOVE INSPIRED BOOKS

ISBN-13: 978-1-335-53898-7

Her Amish Child

Copyright © 2019 by Lenora H. Nazworth

www.Harlequin.com

Printed in U.S.A.

Whosoever shall receive one of such children
in my name, receiveth me: and whosoever
shall receive me, receiveth not me,
but him that sent me.
—*Mark* 9:37

To one of my favorite readers, Patsy Thompson.
Thank you, Miss Patsy, for your encouraging
letters and for your continued prayers!

Chapter One

The gloaming sparkled in a brilliant gold-washed shimmer that covered the sloping valley and glistened through the trees.

Raesha Bawell took a moment to stare out at the end of the day, a sweet Friday in late summer, and sighed with contentment.

It had taken her a long time to reach such contentment.

Even now, with the soft breath of fall hinting in the wind, she still missed her husband, Aaron. Her heart twitched as if it had been pierced but the piercing was now dull and swift.

She'd had to watch him die. How could a woman ever get over that kind of torment? Cancer, the doctors at the big clinic had told them. Too late for surgery or treatments.

Too late for children and laughter, for growing old together, for taking long walks on nights such as this.

Too late.

But never too late to remember joy. She sometimes felt guilty when joy came to her, but tonight she studied the trees and the big creek that moved through the heart of this community. Tonight, she thanked the Lord that she had her mother-in-law, Naomi, to guide her and keep her grounded.

Naomi had been a widow for several years so she knew the pain of losing a dear loved one. Knew it well since she'd also lost two infants at birth. Aaron had been her pride and joy.

But now, Naomi and Raesha had each other.

They worked side by side each day, but Raesha spent a lot of time in the long rectangular building around back of the main house. The Bawell Hat Shop had become more than just hats. They quilted and sewed, canned and cooked, laughed and giggled, and held frolics for their friends almost every month. They had loyal customers, both Amish and Englisch. They'd taken to making not only men's hats, both felt and straw, and bonnets for Amish women and girls, but Easter hats and frilly scarves and caps for tourists, too.

"You don't need to stay here with me,"

Naomi always said. "You are young and full of life. You should get married again."

"I am content," Raesha would always reply.

"You could go back and be with your family. I'm sure they miss you."

"My family is two hours away and they have other children and grandchildren," she always replied. "They know my place is here with you."

Her siblings often came for visits and to see if she wanted to return two counties away and start over there. She did not.

Now as she watched the sunset and thought about the beautiful wedding bonnet she'd made for a young neighbor who was about to become a bride, she knew she *was* content.

And yet, she still longed for a husband and a family.

Raesha turned to go inside and start supper, prayers for comfort foremost in her mind. She had nothing to complain about. The Bawells had built a fine house that kept growing since her in-laws always welcomed nieces and nephews and friends. People had moved in and out of their lives, filling the void after they'd lost two children. The house and outbuildings were neat and symmetrical, steady and solid. From the red big barn that held livestock and equipment to the *grossdaddi haus* beyond the main structure to the big shop that covered the length of the western side of the house to allow for parking, the Bawell place was a showpiece but in a plain, simple way. She and Naomi had a lot of help keeping up this place. Raesha never wanted to live anywhere else.

Turning to go and assist Naomi with lighting the lamps and warming dinner, she heard something round on the other end of the long porch, near the front door. A sound like a kitten meowing.

Listening, Raesha moved across the wraparound porch and turned the corner toward the front of the huge house. Had a stray come looking for milk?

The cry came again. And again. Soon soft wails echoed out over the fields and trees.

Then she saw the basket.

And a little pink foot kicking out in frustration.

Raesha gasped and put a hand to her mouth. A *bobbeli*?

Raesha fell down beside the big, worn basket and saw the pink blankets inside. Covered in those blankets and wearing a tiny pink hat stitched with darker pink roses lay a baby.

"Sis en Maedel." A girl.

A very upset and wailing baby girl.

Grabbing up the basket, Raesha spoke softly

to the baby. "Shh, now. Let's get you inside and see what we have to feed you."

What did they have? Goat's milk. Cow's milk, but no mother's milk. What was she to do? Naomi would know.

Telling herself to stay calm, Raesha lifted up a prayer for help. Then she glanced around, searching for whoever might have left the babe at her door.

But the sunset had changed to dusk and all she saw was the last shifting shadows of the day as darkness settled over the field and valleys of Campton Creek.

Who had abandoned this child?

Please take care of my little girl. I'm sorry but I am not able to do so at this time. Her name is Dinah and I was once Amish.

Naomi squinted down at the kicking baby and then laid the note they'd found inside the basket on the kitchen counter. "I'm *verhuddelt.*"

"I'm confused, too," Raesha replied as she changed the little girl's soiled clothing, glad they had a few baby gowns and such stocked in the shop and some leftover clothing from the comings and goings of relatives. Thankfully, she had found a supply of commercial formula inside the basket, along with a few disposable diapers and some clothing.

They'd warmed a few ounces of the formula and fed it to her after sterilizing a glass baby bottle Naomi had found in the pantry, hoping that would quiet her until they could figure a proper diet.

"Who would abandon a baby?" Raesha asked in between cooing and talking to the tiny infant. "Such a poignant plea in that note."

"And who would leave the babe with us?" Naomi replied, her once-blue eyes now blighted with old age, her face wrinkled but beautiful still. "Do you think she could belong to a relative? We have sheltered so many here."

"I do not know," Raesha replied, her heart already in love with the darling little girl. "She did say she was once Amish. Does that mean she is never coming back?"

Naomi did a thorough once-over of the kicking baby. "The note gave that indication. But this child doesn't look like any of our relatives."

The child had bright hazel eyes and chestnut curls. Raesha checked her over, too. "She looks to be around three or four months, *ja*?"

"'Spect so," Naomi said, a soft smile on her face. "She is pretty. Seems healthy and she did come with a few supplies, but I still cannot understand."

"God's will," Raesha said, thinking they could easily take care of this *bobbeli*.

"Or someone's free will," Naomi replied, her eyes full of concern. "We need to report this to the bishop."

"First thing tomorrow," Raesha said, her heart already breaking.

Of course, they'd keep the baby within the community if she'd truly come from an Amish mother. The Amish did not always bring in Englisch authorities for such things. Someone had left her here for a reason, though. It would be a shame to let this precious child go back out there to someone who didn't want her or to strangers who might not treat her kindly.

"I think her *mamm* left her with us because she wants her to be raised Amish."

"We will pray on this and do what we must in the morning," Naomi said, her tone calm and firm. "For now, little Dinah, you are safe."

Raesha nodded. "*Ja*, you are right. I worry about the mother but we will pray for her, too." She smiled down at the pretty little girl. "Your *mamm* might come back one day."

Naomi patted her hand and then Raesha finished bathing and dressing the baby. Soon after she gave little Dinah the rest of the bottle of formula, the child calmed, her eyes drooping in a drowsy dance, the long lashes fluttering like tiny butterfly wings.

"I'll sit with her," Raesha said. "Once she's asleep, I'll take the basket into my room in case she wakes."

"I'll heat up the stew we had left from yesterday," Naomi replied. "You'll need nourishment."

"What will we do if someone comes for her?" Raesha asked, her heart clenching, her mind whirling with images she couldn't hold.

Naomi laughed. "We've had a lot of experience in dealing with children, 'member? Some would say we are akin to the foster parents who do the same in the Englisch world. Maybe that will work in our favor, *ja*?"

Raesha's heart filled with a new hope. They did have experience and the Amish way was different from the Englisch way. Maybe they could keep this little one a few days longer. Or weeks even. But if the mother gained remorse and returned, they'd have no choice but to let her take the baby. If she would be capable, of course.

"We could have helped the woman if she'd only asked," she said.

"We will do what we can for this one," Naomi said, always relying on the Lord for her strength.

It would be hard to let this precious one go but Raesha knew it was out of her hands. God would give them the answers they needed.

And she'd have to accept that and stay content.

Two days later, Josiah Fisher stared into the early morning sun and wished he could turn back time. But time wasn't his to hold or change. All things in God's time.

He had work to do. He'd arrived in Campton Creek late last night and found a room at a nearby inn but he had checked out early to come here. Now he stood surveying the homestead his family still owned. It was his land now and he planned to fix it up to either stay here and work the land or sell it and go back to Ohio. Most likely the last choice.

Unless…he could find his missing sister. He hoped he'd hear soon from the private investigator he'd hired. He had told the man he was returning to Campton Creek.

Now he wondered if that decision had been wise, but Josie had been seen in this area. And it was time to face his past.

The neglected property looked sad and forlorn next to the big Bawell acreage just across the small shallow stream that trickled down from the big creek. He'd have to survey the burned-out barn and decide how to renovate it and the part of the main house that had also caught fire, but first he needed to alert the neighbors and introduce himself. Two women living alone would wonder who he was and what was going on.

Besides, he hoped to bargain with them about possibly renting some of their equipment. The Amish innkeepers had told him two widows lived on the big place and rented out equipment and such to bring in funding. Josiah counted that tidbit as a blessing.

Turning away from the memories of how his parents had perished in the barn fire that had jumped to the main house, he was glad the local volunteer fire department had managed to save most of the house.

But not the barn. His father had run in to save the animals and his mother had run inside to save her husband.

Or so that was the story he'd heard.

He walked the perimeters of the gutted, jagged building, amazed to see the pink running roses his mother had loved still growing against what was left of the barn.

Placing his hat firmly back on his shaggy hair, Josiah hurried toward the small wooden bridge someone had built over the meandering stream and crossed the pasture toward the

Bawell house. Taking in deep breaths of the crisp early autumn air, he hoped coming back to Campton Creek had been the right thing to do. He wanted to start fresh, but he couldn't do that in the place where he and his sister had been born and raised. Better to fix the place up and sell it so he could finally be free.

Soon he was on the big wraparound porch, the carpenter in him admiring this fine house. He knocked firmly on the solid oak door and waited.

And then he heard the sound of a baby crying.

Was one of the widows a mother?

The door opened and an older woman dressed in brown and wearing a white apron, her *kapp* pinned precisely over her gray hair, nodded to him. "*Gut* day. The shop isn't open yet. If you'd like to wait around by the door—"

"Hello, ma'am," he said, nodding back. "I'm your new neighbor over at the Fisher place. Josiah Fisher. I'm just letting you know I'll be around doing some work and I also…"

He stopped when another woman appeared at the door, holding a baby.

Josiah took in the woman. Pretty and fresh-faced, she had gray eyes full of questions and hair that shined a rich golden brown. She wore a light blue dress with a crisp white apron. His gaze moved from her to the baby. The child's eyes were open and she seemed to be smiling.

Josiah stepped back, shock and joy piercing his soul. "Is that your child?"

The young woman looked confused and frightened. Giving the older woman a long stare, she finally came back to him. "*Neh*, she is not my child."

"Why do you ask?" the older woman said, her shrewd gaze moving over Josiah.

He didn't want to scare the women but he had to know.

"Her bonnet," he said, emotion welling in his throat. "My younger sister, Josie, had a bonnet like that one. Our *mamm* knitted it special for her but never let her wear it much—not plain enough for our *daed*."

He gave the baby another glance that brought on an uncomfortable silence. "I don't mean to stare, but she looks like my sister, same hair color and same eyes."

The woman holding the baby took a step back, something akin to fear and dread in her eyes.

"I didn't mean to frighten you," Josiah said. "It's just that my sister…has been missing for a while now and I'd gotten information that she could be in this area. Seeing the *bobbeli* wearing that little bonnet brought back memories."

The old woman opened the door wide, her eyes filling with recognition. "You're that Josiah. *Joe* they called you sometimes. Your parents were Abram and Sarah Fisher? Used to live across the stream?"

"Yes, ma'am." Josiah lowered his head. "They died in the barn fire ten years ago. Josie was nine and I had just turned eighteen."

Glancing toward the old place, he went on. "I had left to help some relatives in Ohio when I got word of what had happened. I came home and took care of Josie. We moved to Ohio to be near kin but Josie left Ohio a couple years ago during her *rumspringa*."

The women looked at each other and then back to him, sympathy in their eyes.

"*Kumm*," the woman holding the door said. "We will talk about this."

Josiah removed his hat and entered the sunny, warm house and inhaled the homey smells of coffee, bacon and biscuits, his heart bursting with an emotion he'd long ago buried and forgotten.

This house held hope.

Maybe God hadn't sent him here to rebuild the homestead.

Maybe God had nudged him back to Lancaster County to find his missing sister.

Chapter Two

"I'm Naomi Bawell and this is my daughter-in-law, Raesha," Naomi said, guiding Josiah Fisher into the kitchen. "We have fresh coffee and some bacon and biscuits. Are you hungry?"

Josiah noted how she pronounced her name as *Nah-oh-may*. It rang lyrical inside his head. Naomi's hair shined a grayish white but she had eyes of steel.

Josiah's nostrils flared and his stomach growled. "I don't want to be a bother."

"No bother," Naomi said. "Have a seat at the table and we will bring you food."

Josiah nodded. *"Denke."*

He kept glancing at the young woman who held the *bobbeli* so close. She averted her eyes and pressed the baby tight with one arm while she served him coffee with her free hand.

Soon Josiah had a plate loaded with two

fluffy biscuits and three crisp strips of bacon in front of him. But he couldn't take a bite until he knew the truth.

"You said the babe is not yours?"

The room went still. Raesha Bawell's pretty face paled to a porcelain white. She sat down across the table from him, her eyes on the now-sleeping baby in her arms.

"We found her on our porch night before last," she said, her tone low and calm, her gray eyes stormy with emotion. And resolve.

Josiah's heart beat too fast. He took in a breath. "Found her?"

Naomi nodded. "*Ja.* Someone left her in a basket with a few supplies and a note. We got her all fed and cleaned up and we called in the bishop this morning. He agreed she could stay here for a few days to see if her mother returns. If that doesn't happen, we might need to bring in the authorities. We can't harbor a baby that might not be Amish."

"Josie—my sister—is still Amish. She has just lost her way."

Raesha's head came up, her gaze full of determination. "Eat your food, Mr. Fisher. It's growing cold."

Josiah bit into a biscuit, his stomach roiling but hunger overtaking him. Then he took a sip of the strong coffee. He knew they were waiting for him to say what was on all of their minds.

"The bonnet," he finally said. "Could I take a look at it?"

Raesha glanced at her mother-in-law. Naomi nodded. Carefully, she lifted the dainty little knit cap from the baby's head and handed it over to Josiah. Then she rubbed her fingers through the baby's dark curls, her eyes full of sweet joy.

Josiah's heart did something odd. It slipped and stopped, then took off beating again. This woman holding that baby—it was a picture he would always remember. Raesha looked up and into his eyes. The warmth from the baby's head was still on the soft threads of the little bonnet. He clutched the soft, warm fabric while the woman holding the baby watched him in a calm, accepting way.

Then he glanced down at the pink bonnet, his eyes misting when he saw what he'd been looking for. "There," he said, a catch of emotion clogging his throat. "My *mamm* stitched my sister's initials in the tiny cap. DJF. Deidre Josephine Fisher. She did the same with all of our clothes but never made a big deal out of it in front of others since our father did not approve of showing off. Said it made them even more special because they were made with a mother's love."

Rubbing his fingers over the tiny worn cap, he added, "Josie loved that little hat and kept it hidden in her dresser drawer. After the fire, she found it and made sure we took it with our other things to Ohio." Holding tight to the worn knitted wool, he said, "She took it with her when she left."

Raesha let out a sigh that sounded like a sob. "Are you saying you think little Dinah could be your niece?"

Josiah's eyes held hers. "Her name is Dinah?"

"We found the note," Naomi explained. She stood and walked to where a basket sat on a counter. Then she brought him a white piece of paper.

Josiah read the note, blinking back tears of both relief and grief. "My grandmother's name was Dinah," he said. "My sister, Josie, left Ohio two years ago and wound up in Kentucky. She was engaged to an Amish boy there. A *gut* man from what she told me. But I got word she'd broken the engagement and left. That was over a year ago."

Josie's sudden departure from Kentucky had rattled Josiah to the core. She had written that she loved it there and she was very happy. He should have gone to Kentucky with her but he had work to do. They lived off their relatives' kindness and Josiah felt obligated to stay and pay his *onkel* back. But then Josie had gone missing and one of his cousins had accused Josiah of not doing his share of the work. His family had become tired of his leaving to search for Josie.

Now he felt hopeful for the first time in the last year of searching for his sister. Josie could still be nearby.

"I hired a man to help me search," he explained.

"And did this man find anything?"

"He is supposed to get in touch with me when he does. He knows I'm here. He is from this area and came highly recommended."

He hated to hurt Raesha any further but he had to believe what his eyes were telling him. "*Ja*, I do think this *bobbeli* could be my sister's baby. I heard Josie might be headed this way and one reason I came back to Lancaster County was so I could search for her here."

Holding the bonnet tight in his hands, he looked at Raesha. "I might not find my sister but if this is her child, I've found something very precious." Then he handed the bonnet back to Raesha, their eyes meeting. "But I have to believe my sister hoped I would find her baby and that's why she left the child with you."

* * *

Raesha stood and took the cap back from Josiah Fisher, a great tear rending her heart. While she felt for him, she couldn't let him take this babe. He seemed to be a reasonable man. She prayed he'd listen to reason and not demand to take Dinah with him. "We will have to decide how to handle this."

"We should consult someone at the Campton Center," Naomi said, her hands holding tight to her coffee cup. Then she looked at Josiah. "A few months ago, Judy Campton, an Englischer whose husband descended from the founders of Campton Creek, became a widow. She still lives in the Campton house in an apartment over the garage with her friend and assistant, Bettye, but she has opened her big home to the Amish as a community center where qualified Englisch can help us with certain issues. We now have doctors and lawyers and other experts available for no charge there. Even counselors. All volunteers."

Raesha watched Josiah's face and saw his eyes widen. The man was handsome but the intensity in his brown eyes scared her. "Are you saying someone there can counsel us on this situation?"

"*Ja,*" Naomi replied. "Now that we know you might be related to Dinah, we will also seek advice again from the bishop. We already love little Dinah and we will protect her until we know the truth."

Raesha tugged the baby close, the sweet bundle already embedded in her soul. "We will do the right thing but until we can talk to someone, Dinah remains here with us. She will be well taken care of, I can tell you that."

Josiah came out of his chair and put his hand in the pocket of his lightweight work coat and then shoved his hat back on, his eyes full of a troubled regard as he studied her and the baby. "I will call my investigator. I'll have him search for proof."

"If she had the baby in a hospital, there would be a record," Raesha said. "Maybe even a birth certificate."

"That would certainly show proof," Naomi said. "But most Amish don't have official birth certificates. You might check with midwives in the surrounding counties and communities."

Josiah scrubbed a hand down his face. "I do not mean to snatch the child away. I am thankful that she is safe and warm, whoever she belongs to. But that little cap has my sister's initials stitched in the lining."

"It could be someone else's initials," Raesha said, sounding defensive in her own mind.

"I don't think so," he replied. "My *mamm*

went against our father's wishes to make pretty things so she could sell them to help our family. But some she kept. It's clear to me the baby hat belongs to my sister and this child looks like my sister. The note said she was Amish. How can it not be so?"

"It very well could *be so*," Raesha echoed, torn between her own heart's desire and doing the right thing for the baby. "We will have to find out what needs to be done to prove your claims."

Then she softened her stance, hoping to make him understand. "We have taken in lots of young relatives through the years. We are both widows and I am…childless. We will keep Dinah fed and warm and you can visit her anytime you want, ain't so, Mammi Naomi?"

Naomi bobbed her head. "She could not be in a better place for now. What do you know of children, Josiah?"

His dark eyes flared with regret. Shaking his head, he looked at Raesha again. "I know nothing much about children except my sister, but I have no kin left around here. I need to find Josie and hope she'll change her mind about giving up her child. Little Dinah could be my only close relative and she'll need to know that one day."

"Then we will work together to figure this

out," Raesha said, standing her ground. They all knew he couldn't take care of a *bobbeli* right now. "As I said, you are *wilkum* to visit Dinah."

He studied the baby again. "May I hold her? And then, I'll leave. But I'll be glad to go with you to the Campton Center, both of you. We should all be there to talk with someone."

Raesha indicated she agreed. "Then it's settled. We could go later this afternoon. We have a girl who comes to watch the shop when we have to be away."

"I have much to do today," he said. "But I will make time for this. I plan to stay in the house if I can get it fixed up before winter sets in. I need to find lumber and supplies and get the back bedroom fixed, at least."

"Maybe we should wait," Raesha suggested. "Maybe the mother will come back."

"I still need to call the man I hired," he said. "I'll give him this new information and ask him to talk to hospitals and to check as many Amish communities as he can."

"We have a phone in the shop," Raesha said. "Meantime, we have supplies enough for this little ball of energy. I have learned how to make homemade baby formula since she can't be nursed."

"I will consult with the bishop regarding your information," Naomi said to Josiah. "I hope he will agree we need to protect the child first and worry about the rest later."

"I'd feel better if we brought in a midwife," he added as Raesha carefully handed him the baby. "To make sure she is well."

Raesha looked to Naomi. The older woman nodded. "I'll go and get word to Edna Weiller. She lives around the bend. I'll send one of our shop workers over for her."

"Denke." His big hand touched Raesha's when he took Dinah into his arms. Their eyes met and held, causing a keen awareness to envelop her in a warm glow.

"There you go," she said to hide the swirl of disturbing feelings pooling inside her stomach. "Dinah needs to know we will provide for her. She'll need to know her uncle, too."

"If I am truly her uncle," he said, a soft smile on his face as he stared down at the sleeping baby, "I will take good care of her and raise her as my own." Then he handed her back to Raesha. "But maybe I will find my sister and then she can explain all of this—especially how she came about having a baby in the first place."

"I expect she did it the natural way," Naomi said later that day, shaking her head while she rocked Dinah. "If she no longer considers herself Amish, she might not be able to return to the old ways. But if she wants to return, she will have to confess all. Josiah seems to want to find her, regardless."

She paused, her brow furrowing. "His mention of his father brings back some memories. Abram Fisher was very strict and a stickler for following the *Ordnung*."

"There is a reason we have a rulebook," Raesha replied. And yet her heart went out to Josiah and his lost sister. The lost sometimes did return. She prayed he'd find the girl, but that meant Dinah would have to go back to them.

Your will, Lord. Not mine.

Naomi gave Raesha one of her serene stares. "Abram went beyond the rulebook."

"What do you mean?"

Naomi lowered her voice. "He was not above using his physical strength to make his point."

"You mean, he abused his family?"

Naomi nodded. "Sarah never spoke of it, but the proof was in the many bruises we saw. She had a black eye once and said she'd fallen and hit the floor too hard." Gazing down at Dinah, she added, "We mustn't speak of this, of course."

"No. We mustn't," Raesha agreed, her heart hurting for Josiah and Josie. No wonder neither of them had stayed here.

Earlier, Edna Weiller had come by and looked

over little Dinah, examining her from top to bottom. "This child seems fit as a fiddle," the stout woman announced, her blue eyes twinkling while she danced Dinah around. "And probably much better off now that she is with you two."

"We are going to try to find her mother," Raesha had explained. Then she told Edna about Josiah.

Naomi had talked to Bishop King earlier. "The bishop thinks we're doing everything in the right way. But he expects us to alert the authorities if the woman doesn't return in a week or so, to find out what we should do."

"You'll need proof on this Josiah being related," Edna said. "If no proof is found, the Department of Child and Family Services will want to place her with a foster family until they find proof that the mother can't be located or that Josiah Fisher is truly her *onkel*. The sooner you turn her over, the sooner you could have her back. Or he will, at least. But it'll be a long shot and he might be required to go through foster training. Just warning you, but I don't think it will come to that." Her gaze softened. *"Gott segen eich."*

God bless you.

"Denke."

Edna handed the baby back to Raesha. "I can

ask around amid the midwives. See if any of them know of this child being born."

"That would be helpful," Naomi said.

Troubled after Edna left, Raesha scrubbed down the house, made a chicken casserole for supper, and washed a load of clothes and brought them in to finish drying since the sky had darkened and a cold rain seemed to be on the horizon.

But she still couldn't get Josiah Fisher out of her head.

She wanted to *not* like him. But something had happened to her when he'd held that baby. Raesha's heart had felt as if she'd just fallen off a cliff. On the one hand, she prayed the baby wasn't his niece. But there was no denying the strong possibility. Even so, *she* might not be able to keep the child.

She didn't know which would be worse. Watching a stranger remove Dinah from their home or watching Josiah take the baby away but knowing Dinah was right next door. *If* he stayed on the old farm. What if he took the child back to Ohio?

Well, if he did stay here, Raesha could catch glimpses of the child and watch her grow up. Maybe with a new *mamm* if Josiah found a suitable wife. He obviously wasn't married since he had no beard and she didn't see a wife lurking about.

That thought made Raesha rescrub the counter.

"*Ach*, you've done enough. Stop and rest here with Dinah and me," Naomi said, her words low while she smiled down at the sleeping baby.

Dinah had been fussy earlier. Raesha would make the short drive to the general store tomorrow since a baby's needs never ended. For now, they had enough formula to get through the next couple of days. Raesha would have preferred mother's milk, but that wasn't an option. She would buy more supplies to make a more natural formula for little Dinah.

"Stop spluttering and talk to me," Naomi called again.

She and Dinah sat by the heating stove since the day had turned chilly. The afternoon skies looked stormy and the wind blustered around the house. They'd opened the shop for a few hours but had not had a lot of visitors. So they closed the front early and left the workers in the back to their tasks.

People knew to knock on the front door if they needed to pick up an order. They also took orders to the Hartford General Store in town, the closest thing they had to a Pennsylvania Dutch market. Mr. Hartford, an Englischer, sold a lot of Amish wares on consignment and paid them as needed.

When she heard a knock, Raesha jumped. Her nerves were sorely rattled today.

"I'll see who it is," she said, nervous energy bouncing off her.

Raesha opened the door to find Josiah Fisher standing there, wet and shivering in the wind, his hat dripping a pool of water on the porch rug.

"Josiah," she said on a surprised gasp. "*Kumm* inside."

Why was he back so soon? Why did he look so wonderfully good, his dark eyes moving over her in shades of doubt? He had broad shoulders and a sturdy build. Why was she even thinking such things while he stood there in the damp air?

He stepped inside and she shut the door, her arms gathered against her stomach. "Did you need something?"

"I'm sorry to bother you again but it's going to take longer than a day to fix up the house. I was headed back to the inn after I went into town to load some wood, but Mr. Hartford at the general store said you sometimes rent out rooms. I was wondering if I could possibly rent the *grossdaddi haus* out back. It would help me so much to be near my place and I can visit with

Dinah some, too." He paused, his head dipping down. "If that would be all right."

His expression held a longing and a need that Raesha couldn't deny.

But could she tolerate his being so close to Dinah?

And so near to her?

Chapter Three

Josiah took off his hat and hung it on a peg Naomi indicated by the door. Then he sat at the kitchen table while the woman took Dinah with her and Raesha into another room to discuss whether or not they could rent the *grossdaddi haus* to him. He hadn't thought this through and now he regretted blurting out his proposal to Raesha.

She obviously didn't want him around. Did she find him revolting and unappealing or was she afraid he'd take the babe away in the middle of the night?

He'd been so frantic earlier while loading boards at the general store. With the weather turning bad and the idea of either sleeping in a cold house with a burned-out roof on one side or taking his buggy back the fifteen miles to get another room at the inn since he'd given up the one he had, Josiah had voiced his worries to Mr. Hartford.

That's when the kindly storekeeper had suggested this solution. "The Bawell ladies are kind and they have often opened their home to those in need. They make money off their millinery shop and sell other items there— mostly for the tourists who come through. But they need all the income they can find. That's a mighty big place."

Josiah stood and stared out the wide window over the sink. Such a pretty spot, too. He barely remembered the Bawells but then, he'd tried to put his memories of Campton Creek behind him. He did remember that their son, Aaron, maybe a year or so older than Josiah, had spoken to him often at church gatherings and such. Raesha must have come along after Josiah and Josie had moved away.

A big mistake, that. His feisty younger sister had started acting out when she reached her teen years. He'd hoped she'd sown all of her wild oats during her *rumspringa* but Josephine Fisher was determined to see the world outside their small settlement. He still didn't know if she'd ever been baptized.

But he did believe his troubled sister had been running from something.

Well, she'd seen the world all right. His heart

bumped at the weight of seeing that *bobbeli* that only reminded him of his failure as a brother. Was the man she'd been engaged to the father of that baby? Or had she strayed?

If Dinah was even her child, of course.

He'd come back here to salvage the farm and maybe sell it to help pay back his cousin's kindness. But he'd done that only in hopes of finding Josie. But if she'd been here and left this child with these kind women, she'd also done her homework.

What better place to abandon a baby?

He wondered if she'd come home, thinking to open up the house and instead, alone and afraid, had found it wasn't livable. Had she dropped off her child in a fit of despair?

Could she still be in the area?

He'd reached Nathan Craig, a man known for tracking down missing Amish. Nathan had already talked to several people who'd seen a young woman fitting her description and carrying a baby. But she could easily blend in here among the other younger women. Someone could be hiding her. He didn't know and now he had other things to consider. The house repairs and, possibly, an infant niece.

Thinking he'd leave and not bother these women again until they all went to the community center tomorrow, Josiah turned to leave.

"Josiah?"

He pivoted at the door to find Raesha standing at the edge of the big long living room. "I'm sorry," he said. "I was aggravated and cold and hungry earlier. Never mind me asking about staying here. I do not think that's wise."

"We don't mind," she said, but she didn't sound sure. "I will have to clear it with the bishop and we'd lock the door to the long porch that connects the *grossdaddi haus* to this house. We don't use that way much now so it's usually locked anyway. We tend to go out the side door by the shop."

"I would not harm you or bother you," he said, hope gaining speed again. "I won't show up on your doorstep again. I just need a place close by while I rebuild my house."

"I understand," Raesha said. "It makes sense and we do often rent out equipment and the occasional room. We often have relatives visiting for long periods and they find the *grossdaddi haus* comfortable."

"I don't want to impose."

"It's no bother," she said. "But we will have to consider what to do if Dinah is truly your niece."

"I had planned to sell the place, but I wouldn't want to take her away." He paused. "I told my *onkel* and cousins I'd be back. I borrowed traveling money from my *onkel* and one of my cousins is angry with me."

Raesha's expression softened at that. "I'm sorry to hear of your hardship. Maybe you can send them the money even if you decide to stay. It might take longer to pay off but at least they'd know you mean to do so. Once you have your house in order she—Dinah—would be right next door."

He grabbed at hope. And he'd be right next to Raesha. "You could visit her often."

"And watch her if you need us."

They seemed to be reaching a truce of sorts.

Josiah gazed at the woman across the room, their eyes holding with a push and pull that reminded him of a rope tug.

"I did call Mr. Craig. People have seen someone matching her description in town and the woman was carrying a baby. But no one can be sure."

"Then there is hope that she will return," Raesha said. "I pray God will give us insight.

"If your sister comes back, we will do what we can for her," Raesha said, her tone soft and quiet. "You can still do what you set out to do and Naomi and I will continue on."

Josiah nodded and rubbed his face. "This is a *gut* plan, *ja*?"

"That remains to be seen," Raesha replied.

"Meantime, you are here and it's storming out there. You will stay for supper."

"I will?"

She smiled at the surprise in his question. "If you are so inclined."

"I'm inclined," he said. "Whatever's simmering on that stove smells mighty *gut*."

"Then sit by the fire and I'll go and tell Naomi we have reached an agreement. We will discuss the details after supper."

"You are a very forceful woman," he said, moving across to the welcoming heat coming from the woodstove.

"I am a woman on my own with a mother-in-law I hold dear and with way more property than I can handle. I've learned to be forceful. Some frown on that, however."

He smiled. "I'm not one of them."

She inclined her head, her eyes going dark gray in the glow from the gas lamps. Then she turned and went into the other room to get Naomi.

Raesha let out a deep breath. "It's settled."

Naomi watched over Dinah. They'd found a huge straw basket that would make do for a bassinet for now and covered it with blankets so Dinah would be comfortable and safe. It sat by Raesha's bed. She had a comfortable room that held the bed, two side chairs and a large but simply made armoire that had stored her clothes along with Aaron's. His were gone now, donated to someone in need.

The room seemed cheerier with the big basket on the floor, a baby sleeping inside.

Naomi rose from the chair she'd taken near the baby's bed. "*Gut.* Our neighbor is in need. We will help him as we can."

"At what cost?" Raesha asked in a whisper.

"It costs us nothing to be kind," her mother-in-law reminded her.

"But the baby—"

"Is not ours either way."

"You're right," she said, feeling as if she were sitting on a fence and couldn't decide which way to jump. "You're right."

"Let's go and have our supper," Naomi replied, taking Raesha by the hand. "A good meal will ease our concerns and maybe we can get to know Josiah a bit more, ain't so?"

Raesha nodded. "*Ja.* I need to know all kinds of things."

Naomi gave her a knowing look, her shrewd eyes still strong enough to see more than she let on.

"For the *bobbeli*'s sake."

Raesha echoed that. "For Dinah's sake. Nothing more."

But there was a lot more going on here than an abandoned baby sleeping away and a stranger eating supper with them.

Her life had changed dramatically overnight.

But she wasn't so sure she would like this change.

"The meal is wonderful," Josiah said, glancing across the table at Raesha. "Do you share cooking duties?"

Naomi held up a wrinkled hand. "I used to run this kitchen but old age has slowed me down. But Raesha is a fast learner and her mother taught her well before she came to live with us."

"We cook for special occasions and frolics, church gatherings and market days," Raesha said, the coziness of the night making her mellow. "But for the two of us, we measure out and don't waste anything."

"A good rule," Josiah replied. "Josie and I were not the best of cooks but we managed. When we first moved to Ohio, we were both so distraught. We'd lost our parents and our relatives didn't much know what to do with us."

"Did you live with some of them?" Raesha asked, her mind wound tight with so many questions.

"For a while we lived with our uncle but

he had a large family to begin with. I made a little money doing odd jobs and we moved into a small house that my cousin owned near them. That worked for a while but Josie was not happy. It's hard to explain death to a child who is old enough to grasp it but still young enough to want her parents." He took a bite of the chicken casserole and broke off a piece of freshly baked bread. "She only got worse as she grew. I think she'd held a lot inside for a long time. We both had."

"I'm sure you did your best," Naomi said, her tone gentle.

"I tried."

He looked so dejected Raesha again felt an overwhelming sympathy for him. "You were young, too. Did you seek help from the ministers or the bishop?"

"I tried to get Josie more involved in the youth singings and frolics. She always was shy and quiet. She wouldn't speak up and she didn't know how to fight for herself." He looked down at the bread on his plate. "Our *daddi* didn't like women to speak up much."

Naomi shot Raesha a measured glance.

They both knew that the man was the head of the household but what most didn't know or understand was that the woman was the heart of the household and kept things running smoothly, all the while holding things close to her heart and praying to God to show her the strength she needed each day.

"We all have our roles to play," Naomi said.

"*Ja*, and some take their positions very seriously," Raesha replied. "My husband, Aaron, was a *gut* man who followed the tenets of our faith but he was never harsh or cruel."

"Nor was his father, my husband, Hyam Bawell," Naomi said, nodding. "Different people have different ways of doing things."

"I didn't mean to imply I went against my father," Josiah said, clearly shaken. "He took care of us and provided for us. But he never seemed content."

Content.

That word echoed inside Raesha's head. She'd been content a few days ago. Today, her life seemed confusing and unpredictable.

The man sitting across from her wasn't helping matters.

She wondered what would have happened if he hadn't shown up at their door. Or if they'd hidden the baby away until he was gone.

But no, that kind of attitude went against her nature and she was very sure Naomi felt the same way.

"May he rest in peace," she said. Then she looked over at Josiah. "And may you live in peace."

Josiah's eyes widened. "*Denke.* You have both been very kind to me."

After they'd each had a slice of spice cake, Naomi stood. "My bedtime has arrived. I'll help with the dishes and then I'll say goodnight. Raesha, you can give Josiah the keys to the *grossdaddi haus.* I trust him to do what is right."

"And what about the bishop?" Raesha asked. "He still needs to hear what we've planned."

"I will speak again with the bishop tomorrow when we are out and about," Naomi said. She shrugged. "He probably will nod and bless us since he's used to this house being a refuge for those in need."

"Go on to bed, then, and sleep well," Raesha replied. "I'll take care of cleaning up."

"Let me help," Josiah said. He must have seen her shocked expression. "I batch myself. I know how to clean a kitchen."

"That is kind of you," she replied, acutely aware that they were alone but Naomi was in the next room. "Once we're done, I'll take you across the porch and show you where everything is."

His rich brown eyes brightened. "It will be nice to have a dry, clean place to sleep."

They went about their work in silence but Raesha had to wonder what he'd seen and done since he'd been away. Had this lonely, hurting man been sleeping out in the elements? He'd mentioned the inn on the other side of town. But where had he been before then?

Just one of the many mysteries surrounding her handsome new neighbor.

No, make that the handsome single man who would now be staying on her property.

Confusing and unpredictable.

But she couldn't turn back now. She had a child to consider. Tomorrow would the beginning of something new either way.

Chapter Four

"You two go on," Naomi said the next morning. "It's too cold out there for old people and tiny babies."

Raesha glanced from where Naomi sat by the fire holding Dinah, her gaze meeting Josiah's. He stood in the kitchen, waiting with a tight somber apprehension.

He'd knocked on the door bright and early, stating a call had come in to the shop for him. One of the workers saw him outside on the tiny back porch and gave him a message to call back immediately.

"Mr. Craig has news," he said the minute Raesha let him inside. "He will meet me at the Campton Center." Then Josiah had asked if they wanted to go with him.

But Naomi had decided she didn't want to do that.

"Your mother-in-law does bring up a good point," he said now. "It is cold out there and damp at that. You and I can talk to him. We need advice on how to handle this."

Raesha couldn't refuse. They needed to know if Dinah was his niece or not. He had to be there to explain and ply his case and she needed to be there to hear the instructions and see to it they both understood how to proceed. She'd also back him up on his claim. How could she not?

"Well, you certainly do not need to be out in this weather," she told Naomi. "Are you sure you'll be okay here with little Dinah?"

"I'll be just fine," Naomi replied, her eyes on the *bobbeli*. "Dinah and I will have a *gut* talk about life."

"We do have Susan Raber coming to run the shop today," Raesha said, glad she'd been able to send word to their reliable helper. "If you need anything, she will be right next door and she has experience with little ones."

"Ja," Naomi said on a chuckle. "The girl has eight brothers and sisters."

Raesha had long ago learned to ignore the pang of hurt in her heart each time she thought of big families. "That she does, so I shall not worry. Josiah and I will find out what needs to be done and then we'll stop at the general store and get what supplies we might need."

"Don't forget to pick up what we need to make fresh formula," Naomi reminded them, her eyes bright with expectation.

And something else that Raesha hoped Josiah didn't notice.

Naomi loved to try to match Raesha up with eligible men. She tried to be subtle about it, but Raesha had sat through too many painful suppers to miss that gleam in Naomi's kind eyes.

"We will get what we need," Raesha said as she went about gathering her heavy cloak and bonnet. She'd dressed in a dark maroon winter dress and dark sneakers and stockings. This first burst of cold weather had come on suddenly.

Just like the man who was about to escort her to town.

She shouldn't feel so nervous but her jitters were from anticipation and a bit of anxiousness to find out the truth about little Dinah. But she was also nervous about being alone with Josiah. She trusted Josiah and knew he would respect her and keep her safe, but something about going off alone with a man who wasn't her husband did give her pause.

She missed Aaron with the sharpness of a knife carving out her heart, and the guilt she felt at even thinking about Josiah as handsome and strong made her purse her lips and stick as close as she could to her side of the big black covered buggy they used during the winter. Chester, the standardbred horse, was not happy being out in the cold. The gelding snorted his disdain and tossed his dark mane. Maybe the usually docile animal sensed the tension between Raesha and Josiah?

"The Campton Center is in the middle of town," she said to ease that tension. The cold wind whipped at her bonnet and cloak, making Raesha shiver.

She loved spring and summer. Winter, which seemed determined to arrive early, made her sad. Aaron had died a few weeks before Christmas. But this year, they might have a baby in the house. Or nearby at least.

Josiah didn't say much. Was he as wound up as she felt?

"I'm sorry you don't know where you sister is," she said, wishing she could ease that burden. Wishing she knew the truth about this whole unexpected situation.

"I appreciate that but she must be close by." He watched the road for too-fast cars and clicked the reins. Chester pranced and settled into a steady, chopping gait. "I searched for her down in Kentucky but no one knew anything.

The man to whom she was engaged went off on his own to search for her so I didn't even get to talk to him."

"I can't imagine how hard that must be for you," Raesha said. "Naomi and I said a prayer for you and your family last night."

And she'd been in constant prayer since little Dinah had shown up on her doorstep. The adorable girl was so sweet and had such a happy disposition Raesha didn't want to think about having to let her go.

"I came back here to check on the property but mainly to see if Josie might be here," he said, his gaze slipping over her face. "And because a friend of Josie's heard her talking about wanting to come back to Campton Creek and the home she remembered. She was never happy living in Ohio. She's had a hard time of it since our *mamm* and *daed* passed."

"I suspect you have, too," Raesha said before she could stop herself.

"I have at that," he replied, his eyes on the road, his expression stoic and set in stone. "I worked hard for my uncle and cousins but I never did fit in with them. I couldn't find a suitable wife even when they tried to marry me off. Coming back here seemed a good choice since I hoped to find Josie here, too."

So his family had tried to match him with

someone, but had obviously failed. Was he that hard to deal with?

Not from what she'd seen.

"But you've possibly found your young niece."

"Hard to believe but I do hope it's so." He clicked the reins. "I know it is so."

They made it to town and the main thoroughfare, aptly called Creek Road since it followed the many streams jutting from the big meandering creek. Raesha pointed as they passed the Hartford General Store. The building, painted red and trimmed in white, covered a whole block.

"The Campton Center is just around the corner. The big brick house with a clear view of the creek and the other covered bridge that we call the West Bridge."

Josiah nodded, eyeing the massive house on one side and the creek and bridge on the other. "It's smaller than the big bridge to the east."

"*Ja*, the creek deepens there toward the east," she said, going on to explain how a young girl almost drowned there a while back. "Jeremiah Weaver, who returned to us almost two years ago, now teaches swimming lessons for all the *kinder*."

"*Gut* idea," Josiah said as he pulled the buggy in to the designated parking for the Amish across from the Campton Center. "This place is impressive."

"Yes. Mrs. Campton has been generous with our community. She has no living children and her husband, who served in the navy, died last year. They lost their only son when he was off serving the country."

Josiah stared up at the house. "We all have our battles to fight."

Raesha stared over at him and saw the anguish in his expression. She had to wonder what kind of battles he'd fought to return to a place that brought him both good and bad memories.

What if he never found his sister? What if Dinah truly was his niece? Would he take the child and leave again once he'd sold the old place?

He glanced over at her, his eyes holding hers. He seemed to want to say something but she didn't give him time.

"We should get inside."

Josiah nodded and tied up the horse before coming around to offer her his hand.

Raesha let him help her out of the buggy, then she moved ahead of him, his touch burning a reminder throughout her system.

You can't do this. You mustn't get attached to this man. The child needs you. He doesn't.

And I don't need him either.
She'd be wise to remember that.

"Hello, I'm Alisha Braxton."
The young female lawyer smiled and reached out her hand. Josiah removed his hat, and held it against his chest and then shook her hand. Raesha nodded and gave her a smile.

Josiah introduced himself and then turned to Raesha. "This is Raesha Bawell."

The other woman took Raesha's hand. "It's nice to meet you, Mrs. Bawell. I've shopped at your place many times while doing pro bono work here."

"Denke," Raesha said, glancing at the pastoral painting on the wall that depicted an Amish farm in the mist. She recognized the work as belonging to a local Amish woman who painted.

Alisha Braxton had golden blond hair that fell around her shoulders and pretty green eyes that held a strong resolve. She wore a navy blue business suit. "Have a seat and let's see what I can do to help you two. You look like a nice couple. Why do you need legal help?"

Raesha shook her head. "We are not a couple."

Looking confused, the pretty woman with the expressive green eyes laughed. "Oh, I just assumed you might be remarrying, Mrs. Bawell. I'm sorry."

Raesha let out a gasp, a blush heating her face. "No, that is not the case."

Josiah took over. "Mrs. Bawell is my neighbor. We need to find out if the baby she found on her porch is my niece."

The woman's eyes went wide. "Oh, I see." Turning to Raesha, she said, "Let's start at the beginning. You found a baby on your porch? When did this happen? And where is the baby now?"

"Three nights ago. My mother-in-law has the child at my home." Raesha cleared her throat and tried to explain things in chronological order. "We have taken in children before but those were mostly family and friends. But we talked to the bishop and since the note indicated the mother is Amish, he allowed us to keep the child for a while."

"I see," the woman replied. "So why are you here?"

Raesha began to wonder why herself.

But she went on. "Yesterday, Mr. Fisher showed up and he believes, based on her appearance and a baby *kapp* we found in the basket with his sister's initials stitched inside, that the child is his niece."

Glancing at Josiah, she said, "I came here

with him to seek advice and to see what his investigator has found. My mother-in-law has Dinah and we have a woman nearby in our shop if she needs help."

Looking impressed, the young woman nodded, her wavy hair grazing her shoulders. "Who is your investigator, Mr. Fisher?"

"Nathan Craig," Josiah said. "I first contacted him when Josie went missing in Kentucky. But we never found her. When I got word she might be back in this area, I called him again. He is supposed to be good at tracking Amish."

The woman's face went blank but her eyes said a lot that didn't seem in Mr. Craig's favor. "Yes, he is good at that. He used to be Amish."

Raesha let that settle. It happened. People who left somehow always came back around in one way or another. But they didn't always rejoin the Amish community or confess and ask for forgiveness.

"So you know him?" Josiah asked.

"More than I care to admit," the lawyer lady said. "But he is the best at his job. Is he meeting you here?"

"*He* has arrived," a deep voice said from the open door.

"Mr. Craig." Josiah stood and shook the man's hand while Raesha took it all in.

The man looked world-weary, his expression edged with darkness while his brilliant blue eyes burned bright. His gaze moved over them and bounced back to Alisha Braxton and stayed on her for longer than necessary.

"Good to see you again, Alisha," he said.

"I wish I could say the same," Miss Braxton replied.

Raesha noticed the way the lawyer woman said that.

Seemed the pretty female lawyer might have a beef with the handsome private investigator. Raesha hoped their personal differences wouldn't interfere with Josiah's problem.

Maybe Raesha had read too many Amish mysteries.

The man leaned back against a table off to the side, his boots scraping the hardwood floor. "Okay, so let's get to this."

"What have you found?" Josiah asked, the hope in his voice piercing Raesha's resolve.

Mr. Craig reached inside his leather jacket pocket and pulled out a notepad. "Exactly what we needed. A lead on your sister," he said. "According to several people I talked to in another Amish community not far from here, about three months ago a young girl matching Josie's sketched picture was rushed to a nearby hospital where she had a baby girl."

"That's not definitive information," Alisha said. "Amish women about to give birth are rushed to the hospital all the time. It could have been someone who resembled the missing girl."

"Yes, but several people knew of her and said she kept to herself. She was staying at a bed-and-breakfast and the owner verified that and the fact that she was pregnant. She went into labor in the middle of the night. The owner called for an ambulance. I also went to the hospital and asked around."

Standing, he turned to lean against the wall. "They couldn't tell me everything but when I explained this was an Amish girl and that her brother had hired me to find her, the hospital officials verified that a woman matching her description had been a patient there but she'd left without officially checking out."

"Did they verify that she'd had a baby?"

"No."

"What else?" Alisha asked. "Because you always manage to dig information out of people."

"I might have cornered an aide in the maternity ward."

She gave him a stern look. "And what might you have found?"

"I told her the truth. That Mr. Fisher was searching for his sister, and that he was concerned for her safety. The aide verified by nodding to my questions, that a woman named Josie had a baby there and that she'd left without being discharged."

Alisha shook her head. "One day your back-door tactics are going to get you in serious trouble, Nathan."

"I'll take what I can get to help that girl and her child."

Turning to Raesha, Josiah nodded, tears in his eyes. "Dinah is my niece."

Mr. Craig twisted to smile at Alisha Braxton. "While we haven't verified proof yet, Josiah, I believe you're kin to the baby the Bawell women found."

"Does that mean we don't have to report this or send Dinah away?"

Mr. Craig turned to Alisha, lifting his hands up. "Well?"

She glared at him for a moment and then said, "If the mother didn't receive an official certificate at the time of birth, it's going to be hard to prove this. The HIPAA rules won't allow for much more."

"And I can't get access to the birth certificate," Nathan said. "But Josiah could file for a copy at the Department of Vital Records. You have the mother's name and the baby's name. And in the state of Pennsylvania, the father can't even be listed on the birth certificate if they're not married. He has no rights if his name is not on that document."

Crossing her arms, Alisha gave Nathan Craig a heavy appraisal. "He's right there, but none of your tricks, Nathan. This is a serious matter."

"I told you," he explained. "I'm doing this close to the book, but with the Amish, certain English rules don't necessarily apply. The searches are difficult at best."

The lawyer lady's eyebrows went up. "In this case, we have a missing Amish mother fitting the description of Josie Fisher, who left the hospital with her baby in the middle of the night. Most Amish don't have an official birth certificate, and if this was Josie, she obviously didn't take the time to grab one."

"Should I try to get a copy of the original?" Josiah asked.

"We can do it right here, online, since we have most of the information," Mr. Craig said. "If Josie used her own name and recorded the baby's name, it's worth a shot. You can file since you are related and have the same last name."

"I can walk you through it, Mr. Fisher," Alisha Braxton said. "We have to try but it might be hard if the baby wasn't assigned a social security number and you can't provide one."

Josiah bobbed his head. "You see, Josie

wanted me to find the baby. She must have come here to the old place and seen it wasn't livable. Somehow, she knew about the Bawells taking in people. Maybe she wanted to ask for their help and panicked. But she left Dinah, to keep her baby safe."

"She didn't return to the bed-and-breakfast where she'd been staying," Nathan said. "That means she must be moving around. I'll start checking homeless shelters and women's shelters next, with your permission."

Alisha lifted up in her chair. "Okay, your findings give us a strong indication that we're on the right track. Even with access to her medical records, the hospital can't just hand over information. But a birth record would help solidify Dinah staying within the Amish community."

"So she could stay with Josiah?" Raesha asked. "Maybe if Josie knows her child is with her brother, she'll return to Campton Creek."

"I hope so," Alisha said. "Normally, Mr. Fisher, you'd have to file for guardianship, but seeing as your sister is Amish, that makes the baby Amish. And I understand the Amish tend to take care of their own."

Mr. Craig leaned down to stare at Alisha Braxton. "I'm impressed. You rarely veer from the letter of the law."

"Sometimes, the laws become a little gray in certain areas," she explained. "And the Amish are one of those areas." Then she looked at Josiah. "But I expect you to be responsible for this child. The Bawells will help you, because it's the Amish way. But ultimately, the responsibility falls on your shoulders since her mother is missing and, apparently, her father is not legally involved."

Josiah nodded. "I wonder if that's why she ran away. Maybe something happened to the man she was to marry."

"That's a question to ask her if you ever find her," the lawyer said. "I know this is hard on you but the bonnet with the initials is a strong indicator, as is the fact that she left the baby near your old home, with two women known for taking in orphans and people in need. That shows she was thinking of the baby's safety, and you came here not long after she had to have been nearby. She might be keeping tabs on you and could come back on her own."

"So we're all clear?" Josiah asked. "I won't do anything illegal but I want my niece with me."

"You've done everything right, Mr. Fisher," Alisha Braxton said. "Even hiring this irritating man."

"Thank you," the man said, his expression

full of gratitude. Then he looked at Josiah. "But Josiah, your sister is still missing. She allegedly left the hospital at the end of May. Now I can focus on my continuing search, loaded with a lot more information."

"Please keep searching," Josiah said, worry clouding his features. "We will keep Dinah safe but we need to find Josie."

Mr. Craig stood. "Sometimes, people don't want to be found."

Again, a look passed between him and the lady lawyer. *What secrets do they have between them?* Raesha wondered.

Chapter Five

"I have to get back at it," Mr. Craig said while Alisha filed for the birth certificate and explained the process as she went. Glancing at Raesha, he offered his hand. "We weren't formally introduced. I'm Nathan Craig."

"Raesha Bawell," she said, briefly shaking his big hand. "Thank you. Dinah is precious and we so want to keep her safe."

"Now you can do it legally," he replied. "Nice to know Josiah's got some good people to help him."

Alisha stood and scooted around him. "So we don't need DNA and no need to call in social services. You should receive a copy of the birth certificate in a few days, Mr. Fisher. It will arrive at the shop's address. Is there anything else I can help you with?"

"I just need my sister found," Josiah said. *"Denke."*

"I'll do my best," Nathan Craig said. "I'll walk you two out."

Raesha stood and nodded to Alisha. *"Denke."*

"Of course." The other woman's smile held a trace of sadness. Her work had to be difficult.

Giving Alisha a good long glance, she felt Josiah nudging her toward the door where Mr. Craig stood waiting.

"We don't want to get lost on the way out," Josiah said with a smile.

"It is a big place." Alisha followed them out into the long, wide entry hall. "But I'm the first door on the left. Always. Used to be the dining room."

"You've been very helpful," Raesha said.

"I hope this all works in your favor," Alisha replied.

"So do we." Josiah turned, his eyes on Raesha.

Alisha sent a knowing glance to Raesha, matching Raesha's earlier one to her.

Raesha decided Englisch and Amish women had something in common at least.

Trying to understand men.

When they arrived back home, Josiah took care of the buggy and the horses and then turned to stare at Raesha. "Are you sure you want to do this?"

"What do you mean?" she asked, fear clogging her throat.

"I'm asking so much of you already, and now, a little one to watch over and take care of. It's not fair to you."

"It would be unfair for you to have to hire someone else when I am standing right here and I'm able and willing to help for the sake of the child," she retorted, her tone firm. "Now stop your spluttering and let's get inside."

He lowered his head, a smile twitching at his lips.

"Do you find my words amusing, Josiah?"

Lifting his gaze, his eyes filled with mirth. "*Ja*, I do. You are one bossy woman."

She raised her chin. "I have learned to be firm. I employ several people, both men and women. I'm trying to be practical. There is a need and I'm filling it." Then she looked toward the house. "How could I not want to hold Dinah and take care of her? She is beautiful and she needs a woman's touch."

"So you think I can't handle a child on my own?"

"No, I think you should not have to handle this all on your own. We are friends and, for now, neighbors. You are renting rooms in my home. It makes sense to me to leave her with Mammi Naomi and me while you are doing your work." Giving him her best stubborn glare, she added, "Unless you have a plan on how you can do both."

Josiah shook his head. "My only plan was to get her back." Looking sheepish, he said, "I accept your help. I will never question you about this again."

Relief washed over Raesha. "*Gut.* It's early yet but I have not eaten since breakfast. Now let's go in and have some dinner."

"Are you inviting me, then?"

"It seems I am at that. We might as well feed you, too, ain't so?"

"I will do what I can around here to help pay you back," he said, humility coloring the words. "I owe you and Mammi Naomi a great debt."

"We do this out of love," she retorted. "Love for a helpless man." Then her lips crinkled. "And for a helpless friend, too, it seems."

Josiah's expression changed from agony to happiness again. "I am helpless in this area and many others, that is true. But I believe your good habits will rub off on me."

"We will see about that," Raesha replied before marching past him to get out of the brisk wind.

Once there, she fussed with sandwiches made with fresh bread and juicy baked ham and fresh cheese. She poured tea and heated up the coffee on the big stove. She placed fruit and cookies on the table. But her eyes wandered to the little crib in the corner over and over.

Naomi glanced from her spot cutting up fruit to Raesha and then back to Josiah. "I am so proud that Dinah can stay with us."

"I thank God," Josiah said, his gaze following Raesha. She wanted this, too, but he wondered what would happen if she got too attached to his niece. How could he take the child away if Raesha didn't want to let her go?

She is my kin, he reminded himself. *It is my choice.* He'd come here determined to fix the place up and sell it so he could pay back some of the money his uncle had loaned him to find Josie. Or maybe he'd used that as an excuse since he needed to get away from his relatives for a while. Not run away, but take some time. He'd never really taken time after his parents died to mourn them and the life they should have had here, to console himself and to do right by Josie. He'd dragged her away, unable to think straight.

Now he wondered if God hadn't nudged him

here for many reasons. Raesha would make a good mother to any child.

Did he want to stay? Could he? Too many questions.

The weather cleared, warming but still with a nip in the air and the sky shining a brilliant blue in the sun. Early on Sunday morning, they all bundled up to head to church, which would take place at Bishop King's house. Here, church rotated from houses or farms to barns and basements, depending on who could accommodate the congregations.

Thinking about how they'd received stares and raised eyebrows during their quick trip through the general store yesterday, Raesha was quiet as she got in the buggy and took Dinah from Josiah. To distract herself, she made sure the baby had plenty of blankets and that her head was covered.

Josiah checked on Dinah. "She's always so happy."

The little girl smiled a lot, which made Raesha smile, too. "*Ja*, such a good girl."

Josiah's fingers briefly touching hers and his solemn eyes glancing over her face made her only too aware of the man.

Last night, they all sat around the woodstove, taking turns holding Dinah.

Naomi cooed and talked to the little one, promising that no matter what happened they had all been blessed by Dinah's presence in their home. "*Gott* will be with you."

Josiah then held the baby close, not speaking. Just staring down at her with awe. Finally, he'd kissed her little forehead, tears in his eyes. "*Gott* will return your *mamm* to me, I pray. His will and my prayers. Your mother would want it so."

He'd looked up and into Raesha's eyes, a binding connecting them with an invisible thread. When her turn to hold Dinah had come, she blinked back tears and refused to look over at Josiah.

But she voiced what they were all thinking. "You are loved, little one. We will keep that love even if you have to move far away."

Now Raesha's heart bumped each time the buggy hit a rut in the road. How could she love someone she'd known for only a week? Was this how it felt to have a child of your own? It shouldn't hurt this much to think of letting Dinah go. But the choice would not be hers.

Josiah would have to decide what to do, even if his sister was found.

It would be an honor to help him take care of Dinah until that time. If Josie never returned, he'd need even more help.

But what if he decided he didn't want them in his niece's life? He'd indicated he might allow them to help, but what if he changed his mind once he knew he truly was Dinah's *onkel*? Too many questions.

Naomi remained calm and serene, her gaze admiring the countryside. She was good at waiting on the Lord. Raesha should learn from her but patience and waiting had never been her strong points.

Raesha missed her own mother. Ida Hostetler had died when Raesha was a teenager and her father, Robert, had passed not long after she'd married Aaron and moved away. She had three siblings. An older brother, Amos, who lived with his family in the house where they'd all grown up, and Emma and Becca, twins who lived right next to each other. They all had children and she loved helping to take care of her three nieces and two nephews when she went to visit or when they came here.

She hadn't told any of them about little Dinah yet, of course. But her sisters would come calling sooner or later and they'd be shocked to find a baby in the house. Or worse, even though they lived in another community, word could get out to her family no matter how quiet Josiah and she wanted to keep this until they knew what would happen next. They'd certainly have questions regarding Josiah living on the Bawell property.

"Hold on," Josiah said when a vehicle came up behind them. "We will let the Englischer get by since he seems in such a hurry."

He moved the buggy to the side, careful and considerate.

He looked handsome in his clean black pants and white shirt, his dark hair curly underneath his black hat. His jacket was clean and he smelled of fresh soap. Apparently, he was enjoying living in the *grossdaddi haus*.

She shouldn't be admiring the man guiding Chester, and yet she couldn't help it. She'd been isolated and in mourning for so long, she had not realized that her heart had shriveled to almost nothing. Little Dinah had brought her back to life, and now Josiah was adding more beats to her heart, too.

She'd been content.

She needed to remember that and not jump beyond content. But being content wasn't as pleasant as the many feelings stirring inside her heart right now.

She couldn't allow those feelings to take over.

Not until they grew to know each other more and she might have some hope to add to her blossoming happiness.

They made it to the King place and after

securing Chester at the hitching rail, Josiah helped her down and then assisted Naomi.

Naomi smiled and thanked him, her eyes twinkling. How could she be so chirpy when their life had become so shaken and changed?

I need to have a stronger faith, Raesha reminded herself. If Naomi did worry, she sure hid it well enough. Raesha's emotions usually came out in her expressions, according to her bossy sisters.

She'd work on controlling her feelings this morning. For Dinah's sake, at least. People would be curious and they'd all agreed to speak the truth.

Once they were out of the buggy, they made their way to the basement of the big house, where the service would take place. Naomi took the foods they'd prepared earlier and went to a gathering of older women, all of them spluttering on about the meal they'd all share later. One of the women took the pickled beets and coconut pie into the kitchen.

Raesha held Dinah tight and waved to some approaching friends.

The men would go in first, followed by the younger boys.

Josiah stood to the side, looking lost. But some of the people he'd met in town, including Jeremiah Weaver, who'd returned to Campton

Creek a couple of years ago, came up to Josiah and guided him into the service. He glanced back, his expression hard to read. Did he worry about the *bobbeli*?

A group of women came up and started admiring Dinah.

"So it's true, then?" Beth Weaver asked, smiling. "You found a baby on your porch?"

"That is true," Raesha replied, smiling at Dinah's wide-eyed expression. "But her *onkel* is renting rooms from us and we are helping him out while he rebuilds his place."

"Was that him?" someone else asked, pointing to where the men were moving slowly down into the open basement doors. "The new fellow who walked in with the others?"

"His name is Josiah Fisher," she explained. "He came here to fix up his family farm and maybe sell it but he also came back to find his younger sister. Now he will have this little one to think about, too."

"Where *is* her mother?" nosy Rebecca Lantz asked, her smile prim while her eyes glistened for details.

"She had to go away for a while."

"I heard she left the babe. Abandoned her own child. If she does come back, she might have a ban on her. She's not even from our district."

"But they used to live here," someone replied.

"Josiah has someone searching for her," Raesha explained, her tone firm and calm. "I ask that you pray for both of them, Rebecca. You are kind to worry so about someone you don't even know. Until she returns, Mammi Naomi and I are helping with the baby, with the bishop's approval. It's the right thing to do, don't you agree?"

Rebecca huffed a breath, but with the other women watching her with amused expressions, she nodded. "Of course I'll pray for them. That is a cute baby girl and yes, you always do the right thing, Raesha."

Leave it to Rebecca to wrap an insult inside a compliment.

Naomi came up and greeted everyone and then said, *"Gott verlosst die Seine nicht."*

God does not abandon His own.

Rebecca smiled and walked away with a flip of her skirt.

"I pray so, if it is God's will," Naomi said. "I pray Josie will find her way back to this child and her brother."

They made it through the long service but Raesha had to take Dinah upstairs once to feed her and change her nappy. No one seemed that concerned since the truth had come out. Just another person needing the Bawell widows.

Some of the teen girls passed the baby around and helped out so Raesha could eat. They all loved Dinah.

But Raesha knew taking care of this child and standing by this man went beyond her sense of duty.

Once the meal was over and they were heading home, Naomi sat with Raesha inside the buggy. Her mother-in-law took Raesha's hand and held it tightly to hers. "You will make a good *mudder* someday."

Raesha prayed that so, too. She wanted Dinah with a heart that burned to love someone. "One day. But I have to remind myself that this child does not belong to me."

"Are you going to be able to deal with whatever might come?"

"I will," Raesha said. "You know I will."

"I think the Lord has plans for you," Naomi replied with a pleased smile.

As she watched the broad shoulders of the man who'd come so unexpectedly into their lives right on the heels of finding the babe on her doorstep, Raesha had to see God working on all of them in some way.

What are You trying to teach me, Lord?

How could her heart be so full and yet so completely empty at the same time? She could see everything just out of her reach and it seemed she'd lose out yet again.

But Josiah aimed to stay around a while to get the old farm back into shape and to wait for word on his sister. She had a little time with the baby yet. She would cherish each moment for the gift given to her.

A lot could happen before the year was out. She'd just have to wait.

Be still, she told herself. *Just be still.*

It would be a long winter and a lonely one if Dinah and Josiah had to leave them.

Chapter Six

Josiah looked up a couple of days later to find a convoy of buggies headed up the rutted lane to the old farm. Surprised, he walked to the front of the run-down house and watched as, one by one, the men in the buggies pulled up and got out with tools and supplies.

"What is this?" he asked as one of the men introduced himself as Samuel Troyer. Josiah nodded and shook his hand. "You are one of the ministers for this district, *ja*?"

"That is correct," Samuel said. "Jeremiah Weaver is my son-in-law and he mentioned you might need some help. He'll be here later."

Josiah lowered his head. He knew this was the Amish way but he still felt inadequate. He should have come back here long ago to take care of this place and face the harsh reality of his past. But he'd tried to raise his sister and he had wanted to protect his parents' memory. Instead, this place shouted loud and clear about the unhappy times here.

"I would appreciate the help, *ja*."

"Winter will set in soon," Samuel reminded him. "You'll need the place strong if you aim to sell it."

"Word travels in this community," Josiah said. "I haven't decided what to do but the house needs repairing, no matter."

"So you'll be here a while, then?"

Josiah didn't want to blurt out his business so he just nodded again. "I'm staying at the Bawell place." He motioned toward the footbridge. "In the *grossdaddi haus*."

"So I heard. The Bawell women are good landlords, ain't so?"

"They have been kind to me," Josiah replied. "They seem to take in strays from what they've told me."

"They are good women, caring and loving. And smart, businesswise, too," Samuel replied.

Samuel Troyer had to already know all about his situation but the other man wouldn't question him outright. He did speak of his hopes of Josie returning. In his heart, he felt God had led him home.

"We will pray for you, Josiah," Mr. Troyer said. "And for your lost sister."

"*Denke* for coming," Josiah said to change the subject. "I'll take all winter if I do this alone."

Soon he was shaking hands and being introduced to a dozen or so able-bodied men who'd come to help him renovate the house.

"The barn will be next," Samuel told him when they took a break to warm themselves by a fire someone had started in an open area. "Hopefully, we can get it repaired and built before the weather takes a turn."

"I am mighty obliged," Josiah said as they went back to work on the side of the small two-storied house that the fire had gutted. Soon they had the charred remains of the old walls torn away and were working to rebuild from the floor up.

The work went quickly and got done much faster than if Josiah had tried to do it all on his own. He'd torn out a lot of rotting, scorched wood already, his body willing since it kept his mind off Dinah and his missing sister. And off the woman across the way who'd been so kind to him.

Raesha's smile shined in his mind like a beacon. He couldn't seem to get her out of his head. But then, it would be hard to avoid her if he tried.

At the end of the last few days, she'd either

invited him to supper or brought him a plate. She was shy and reserved but she didn't have any qualms about speaking her mind either.

"The Bawells stay busy," Samuel said while they measured and hammered. "The hat shop has a long history here. Mrs. Bawell's husband and son ran it until… Mr. Bawell passed. Then Aaron and Mrs. Bawell did their best to keep it going. When Raesha came into the family, she dived right in and made a few suggestions to add this and that. She learned all about hat-making and suggested that Aaron hire extra help."

"Wise woman," Josiah replied, careful not to grin too much since he'd seen that feisty side of her. "They do seem to stay busy and they have given work to others."

"Busy, kind and she's single."

Josiah couldn't hide the grin now. "*Ja*, I noticed that."

"And pleasant to look at."

"Noticed that, too."

Samuel chuckled. "I will comment no further on that subject."

"Duly noted." They continued in a pleasant silence until it was time to find some dinner.

"My wife and daughter packed us a meal," Samuel said. "And the others brought their own dinner, too. Let's sit by the fire and eat."

Josiah didn't argue with that. He'd had an egg

and toast in his temporary place this morning. Soon, they were sitting on logs eating roast beef sandwiches made with freshly baked bread and fried apple pies that reminded him of his own *mamm*.

Josiah couldn't help but glance at the big place across the way. Part of Samuel's job as an elder had to be placing people together. Did he think Josiah and Raesha would make a good match?

Josiah didn't know how to go about courting a woman. He'd tried a few times back in Ohio, but he'd always been an outsider there. He didn't have a way with women. Too grumpy and shy, one had told him. Too moody, another had confessed.

Staring out at the pastures, he noticed hay bales stored near barns and plowed, fallow ground that would go dormant during the winter. Past the pastures and hills, he could see the waters of the big creek.

"It's nice here," he said. "I'd forgotten how nice."

"You don't have to sell," Samuel pointed out. "The land on this place just needs tending and clearing. Come spring, you could have it in good shape for planting."

"I know. But I owe my uncle and cousins so much. I thought I'd go back to Ohio and pay them back by helping them as much as I can."

But first, he needed to find Josie. So many questions. If he couldn't find her, and if Dinah would be his to raise, he'd have to decide if he should take her to Ohio or stay here. He'd have plenty of help back in Ohio, but would his strict uncle even allow the child to live there? Would the community accept her without question?

Thinking about Raesha next door didn't help his confusion.

"I'd think you've paid that debt," Samuel said, regarding his return to Ohio. "If you worked hard for your kin I doubt they expect more. Surely they'd understand why you want to come back to your home."

He couldn't argue with that, but Josiah had a need to pay his family back, whether with money or hard work or both. They'd tried to match him to a good woman but none of them worked out. He left on bad terms with his uncle because he refused to marry any of his hand-picked choices. Maybe a baby would make Josiah come to his senses and listen to his uncle's wishes. He'd need a mother for Dinah.

He thought of Raesha again.

"Can I tell you a story?" he asked Samuel, his heart burning with a longing to unburden himself.

"I like to hear a good story," the older man said on a quiet, knowing note.

Before long, Josiah had spilled the whole truth of his past and what little he knew of his sister's life. The other men had discreetly talked in clusters while he talked quietly to Samuel.

Finally, he finished and stared down at his brogans. "So you see, I have much to consider. The child is my niece and I have an obligation to provide for her and raise her. If I find my sister and she is all right, she can be a mother to her child. But first, we'd have to go before the bishop and see how to handle this situation. I won't be able to stay here if Josie is shunned."

"And how will you be received back in Ohio?" Samuel asked.

Josiah lifted his head. "It would not be *gut*, but I won't abandon my sister or her child."

"You do have a lot to consider," Samuel replied. "But if you find Josephine and she confesses all and asks for forgiveness, I believe you could live here with her. Quietly and she'd have to find a husband soon enough."

"But you can't be sure how anyone will react," Josiah said.

"No. It would be up to the bishop and the other ministers," Samuel replied. "And it will be *Gott*'s will."

"I felt a tugging to come home," Josiah admitted. "I think Josie is nearby."

"You might well be right on that," Samuel

said. "Let's get your home ready in case she is close and waiting. I think the girl needs her home back, *ja*?"

Josiah nodded, too choked up to speak. He admired Samuel's kind nature and understanding, wise counsel. He liked Jeremiah Weaver, too. He'd heard how Jeremiah had left but returned and was now back in the Amish way.

He wanted that for Josie, if it wasn't too late.

Maybe he could have a new life here in the place he'd never wanted to see again. In a house that held horrible memories, maybe through restoration and redemption he could create new memories.

And…he might be able to do that with the woman who lived next door.

"There is much going on next door," Naomi said from her chair by the side window.

Raesha turned from finishing the last of the apple and sweet potato pies she'd been baking all morning. She had to go to the shop in a few minutes to relieve Susan. The girl's *mamm* was sick and Susan was needed to help with the younger children.

"I saw the buggies arriving earlier." Handing Naomi her afternoon tea, Raesha glanced out the window. "They have done a lot since early this morning."

"That could be a nice house. Small but cozy. Just needs some love," Naomi said, her hand holding the cup underneath the plain white teacup.

"Tell me what you remember," Raesha said. "Josiah is such a quiet, polite man. I can't see him coming from a *daed* who would abuse his family."

"Josiah is trying to be the opposite of his father," Naomi replied with a nod. "He doesn't seem to invite confrontation. He mentions trying to please his uncle and cousins but I wonder if he ever tried to stand firm with them."

"Do you think he's weak, then?" Raesha brought her own tea over and sat for a moment, her mind on Josiah and the odd feelings he brought out in her. Little Dinah slept snugly in her crib, only reminding Raesha of him.

"No, not weak. Trying to hold it all in, trying hard to be a *gut* man and not cause trouble. But as you've seen, he will fight for his own."

Raesha believed that and she didn't consider Josiah as weak. He'd been working hard to find his sister and he was determined to raise little Dinah, if need be. He'd come home to do what needed to be done.

"What happens if he becomes weary of holding things inside?" Raesha asked.

"He will have to come to terms with that,"

Naomi replied. "He will need to listen to the Lord and be steady in his ways."

"Josiah has a lot on his mind," Raesha said, getting up. "But seeing the work our community has helped him with today should ease his troubles, *ja*?"

"I believe so," Naomi replied. "Now it's time for my nap. I will pray for our Dinah before I shut my eyes."

"Pray that she stays asleep while you nap," Raesha said. "Josiah has been doing a good job with her when he comes to fetch her each night. I had to show him how to change her diapers. He made a funny face but he is a quick learner."

"He makes you laugh," Naomi noted.

"He's a funny man."

Raesha helped her mother-in-law to her bedroom and made sure she had a warm blanket. "Rest, Mammi," she said with a tenderness that made Naomi smile.

"Denke." Naomi eased into the covers and then added, "You do know you are not required to stay here with me."

"I do know that since you remind me at least once a week," Raesha replied. "Are you trying to get rid of me?"

"Not at all," Naomi said, a playful slap warming Raesha's hand. "But you are young yet. You should get out and about more."

"And for what reason would I need to be out and about?"

"I can see a couple reasons," Naomi replied. Then she shut her eyes, her smile still intact.

Raesha gathered her things to take to the shop, mindful that she'd be going back and forth to keep an eye on the baby and Naomi. In the last week, she hadn't been on task so she had a lot to catch up on. Naomi was still good with needles, so she helped with making bonnets and children's hats and she was wonderful with embroidery, too. But her mother-in-law was declining so Raesha tried to encourage her to rest after dinner each day.

Hopefully, both baby and Mammi would sleep until she unloaded her things, checked on the shop and hurried back to the house. She'd never realized how taking care of a little one changed everything.

And now, she had Naomi hinting at matchmaking.

Naomi worried about Raesha's future. Even though they both knew God had a plan for them, her beloved mother-in-law wanted to know she would be safe and taken care of once Naomi was gone.

Raesha didn't want to think that far ahead. This big house would be so empty without Naomi. She had always been the heart of this house, loving and open and kind. Raesha wanted to be the same but it would be hard, going it alone. She'd keep the shop up and running and she'd bring in people to keep her company. She had so much love to give. Maybe that was why she enjoyed being a shopkeeper and hatmaker. Her work involved being around others.

But she wouldn't make a move until she knew what would become of baby Dinah. The baby had been in her thoughts all week as she trained Josiah on how to handle a tiny child. He wanted the responsibility, took it in stride and he'd insisted on doing his part by taking Dinah to the *grossdaddi haus* with him each night.

"We are getting to know each other," he told Raesha one early morning. "I cannot thank you enough for watching her during the day."

It was easy to see the baby was related to him. Dinah's eyes looked a lot like his, golden brown at times and a richer brown at other times. Always changing.

"It is a pleasure," she'd assured him. "Dinah is a bundle of sweetness."

At least she could hold on to the child until they could find her real mother.

Raesha prayed about that, too. Josie had to be alive and safe. Josiah would be heartbroken if anything bad had happened to his sister.

He needed to know the truth. What had caused Josie to run away and have a baby all on her own?

Chapter Seven

The next day, Raesha sat at the tall stool behind the counter in the front of the hat shop, making a list of all the winter chores that had to be done before the first snowfall.

A friend had come to visit Naomi and assured Raesha she'd be happy to sit with Dinah for a couple of hours, too.

That left time for Raesha to focus on business, something she'd found soothing in the months after Aaron had died.

Earlier in the season the hay had been dried, baled and stacked by the barn. Some of it was already stored in the hayloft, ready to use. The two men who farmed the land for them would move the rest to the barn before hard winter set in. The fences had been checked and mended and the livestock—just the horses, a few cows and some goats—were in good shape.

She'd have to make sure the hay cart was in working order and the draft horses had sturdy harnesses. There was wood to gather and cut for the stoves and they'd need to make sure they had a winter supply of propane for the shop. While they had a phone in the shop, they used it only for business or emergencies. She filed the handwritten invoices on any transactions and worked with a neighbor who was an accountant to keep business in order.

The phone rang, causing her head to come up. "Bawell Hat Shop. How may I help you?"

After taking an order for two felt hats, with measurements written down by hand on the invoice pad, she said, "*Denke.* I will get these back to the sewing room today."

Then an Englischer came in looking for shawls and bonnets.

"I want something handmade and Amish," the robust woman said, waving her hand in the air. "I admire the quality of these quilts, too. Maybe I should buy one of those."

Thirty minutes later, she left happy with two shawls, three bonnets and a log cabin quilt. Raesha waved goodbye to the spry woman and took a sip of her lukewarm tea, her gaze moving over the long, wide retail building. Two doors with glass windows centered the long planked-floor room. Rows and rows of hats lined the walls on one side, while clothing and quilts covered the other side. Then a long row of open shelves moved from the heavy oak purchase counter centered in front of the doors to both sides of the room. Those shelves were full of jams, jellies, breads and pastries, most provided by local Amish women trying to make some spending money. Ava Jane Weaver had a whole shelf of her wonderful sweets, mostly cakes and pies and muffins. She sold her bakery goods here and at the Hartford General Store in town.

Then there were the handmade items that the Englischers loved. Crocheted and knitted caps and hats in all sizes, similar to the pink one little Dinah had been wearing.

Her heart pierced, thinking about how much she missed the *bobbeli* when she came here to work. Lifting her gaze over the tiny clothing and head covers, she touched her own tummy and wondered what God's plan was for her.

Will You leave Dinah to us, Father?

Shaking her head, she skimmed the walls lined with landscape paintings and colorful wooden signs that held Amish proverbs and verses of Scripture.

The hat shop had come a long way in the last ten or so years. But it felt big and lonely without her Aaron and his *daed*. Business was slow but it would pick back up with the Harvest Festival in a few weeks and the holidays after that.

Thinking she could set up a corner for Dinah and bring the baby here with her some days, Raesha made notes on her big calendar, trying to mark down all the things she needed to supervise. She and Naomi employed a dozen or so people. It took that many to keep things running smoothly here. One reason she didn't have time for courting.

Josiah came to mind and she pushed his image away and made a note to check the employee gathering room.

They had a small efficiency kitchen in the back of the shop, so employees could take breaks and eat meals, especially during the busy Christmas season and the high tourist seasons of spring through fall. Winter was for repairing things, building up inventory and making sure everything was in order for next year, and they had to prepare for the busy weeks before Christmas.

Aaron used to help her with such chores. He'd get the wood gathered and stacked and, together, they'd make sure the outbuildings and stables were secure and ready for winter. He'd let the horses out for air, their winter coats keeping them warm while they ran in the snow.

She could see him out there now, laughing

at the big draft horses or trying to encourage Chester to come out and play. Aaron would have been the best father. Watching how gentle he was with the animals had always made her smile.

He'd turn and motion for her. "*Kumm* and play. *Kumm*, Raesha."

She thought about the man living on the property now. Josiah had kept his distance the last few days. Other than taking him meals when he came to get Dinah, she rarely saw him. He was up before dawn, handing her the baby with few words exchanged, then heading to work on the house next door. But she'd noticed little things he'd done here, too.

The big barn looked cleaner and better organized and the horses had fresh water and feed before she could even get out there to take care of them. Josiah worked hard and kept his rooms clean, gathered his own laundry and tried to wash his own clothes. But Naomi and Raesha had insisted it was no bother to throw his clothes in with theirs. During the winter months, they stretched a line across the basement from wall to wall and hung clothes there to dry. His were lined up on the end where he could find them when he needed them.

But it had been nice, seeing a man's clothing hanging there not far from her own. Nice, but she felt as if she was betraying her beloved Aaron.

"I want you to be happy," he'd told her many times. "Find a *gut* man to take care of you and Mamm. Promise me."

"I only want you. Stop spluttering about that. I'll never love another man."

"You will have me always. But I want you to be happy."

Wiping at her eyes, Raesha had tried to be happy. She'd been content and settled and she loved her work and she loved Naomi. Her life had become complacent and constant.

And then little Dinah had come along, followed by Josiah Fisher. Now she was restless and unsettled, that longing she'd tried so hard to temper piercing at her heart and reminding her of all she had lost.

He might be avoiding her, but Raesha couldn't stop thinking about Josiah. Which only made her miss Aaron even more.

While the tree line sheltered most of the Fisher property, she could catch glimpses of Josiah and the various neighbors who stopped by to help when they could. The stream of able-bodied men had been constant. That was the Amish way. The brethren needed help and they came and worked together. Josiah might think he didn't belong, but he was a child of God. He belonged to the Lord and that made him belong to this community.

The door to the shop opened and Susan rushed in. "I'm back. And happy to say everyone at our house is now well." Glancing around, the young girl heaved a sigh. "Ah, peace and quiet."

"*Gut* to see you and so bright and cheery on this chilly morning, too," Raesha said, glad to have her thoughts taken away from Josiah. "Blessing on your family. I hope they all stay well."

Susan's sandy-colored hair was covered with a dark winter bonnet that had been made here in the shop. "I'm glad to be away from the *kinder* for a while," she admitted as she took off her heavy gray cloak. "Mamm says to tell you hello."

"Your mother is kind," Raesha replied, wishing with all her heart she had a big family to fuss over.

Susan fussed with her apron pins and then straightened her prayer *kapp*. "And she wants details on your new boarder."

Raesha chuckled. "I think the word is out. Mr. Hartford gossips like a chattering *gross-mammi*."

"And knows all the gossips, too," Susan said,

nodding. "But we are curious. I hear he's tall and fiercely handsome."

"He is tall," Raesha said. "And moderately nice looking."

"And single."

"So I'm told."

"You know more than you're letting on."

"I won't gossip about Josiah. He is a *gut* man."

"We have no need to gossip," Susan said with a jaunty grin. "But you do need to tell me everything."

Raesha listened to the steam machines in the back of the building, followed by the hum of the two Singer sewing machines. She had four workers here today. They had to stay ahead of the Christmas season, when tourists would come by and when customers would want new hats to give as gifts.

Susan glanced toward the big double doors to the factory. "Do you not want anyone to know you have a crush on him?"

"I do not have a crush on him," Raesha denied a little too quickly. "That's ridiculous. I only just met the man."

"Right," Susan said, her cornflower blue eyes bright, her high cheeks rosy from the cold.

Raesha shot her a wry smile. "Okay, then, do you not have a crush on Daniel King?"

"Shh." Susan put a finger to her lips. "He's working today."

"I know he's working," Raesha replied on a smug note. "Since I'm his boss." Then she grinned. "And I'm thinking that is why you couldn't wait to get back to work, too."

Susan blushed, a sheepish smile broadening her heart-shaped face. "Let's call it even and I will be quiet."

"I think that is the best solution," Raesha replied.

But she had to wonder. Did everyone in Campton Creek know her heart? What kind of rumors were flying around? Maybe she should talk to Josiah about the gossip going around, so he could speak for himself. And leave her out of it.

Although, she was pretty much in the thick of it now.

Susan hurried by with a duster. "The midwife told my *mamm*. That's how I found out about him. And the baby, too, of course."

Raesha couldn't deny the truth but she wished Edna didn't prattle so. "The bishop knows of the situation but we were trying to keep it normal for the *bobbeli*'s sake. And because Josiah is concerned about his missing sister."

"There's a missing sister?"

"You already know that, I'm thinking." Raesha slapped a hand over her mouth. "Now I have to tell you everything to set things straight."

Susan nodded, her expression serious now. "I do believe you need to tell someone since I hear mixed messages. Seems a lot has happened over this last week."

Raesha wanted to tell her friend that her whole world had been turned upside down and she needed to share how her heart had beat strongly again after holding little Dinah. But she would cherish those thoughts and keep them to herself.

"When we take dinner," she said, "I'll explain but, Susan, I do not want gossip to spread. I'll tell you the truth but I need you to not repeat it. It's getting out of hand as it is."

"I will do so, all joking aside," Susan replied. "I have never broken the confidences we share during work time."

"Nor have I," Raesha replied, the unspoken truce between them now stated. "It's *gut* to have a friend I can trust."

"*Ja*, and it's good to have an adult to talk to," Susan replied with a jaunty smile.

The girl had a strong sense of righteousness. She and Raesha shared a lot of woman talk. Raesha knew she could trust Susan.

"Denke," she said. "Now I have busy work on the accounts."

"And I have to dust and polish," Susan replied. "And check on the workroom to see if anyone needs water or coffee."

"You mean Daniel King, *ja*?"

"I said everyone," Susan replied with her hands on her hips.

Two hours later, the phone rang and Raesha picked it up, expecting an order from a customer.

But her heart stopped when she heard the voice on the other end of the phone.

"Raesha, it's Edna Weiller. I asked around about Josephine Fisher and my friend Martha Pierce, who lives in the Goldfield Orchard District, remembers helping a girl who was pregnant and working at a bakery. The girl got dizzy and Martha checked her over and told her she was near term, suggested she get off her feet for a few hours. She wore Englisch attire and stayed at the Goldfield B and B."

Goldfield Orchard? Mr. Craig had mentioned he'd talked to people in a community about two hours from Campton Creek.

Raesha took a breath. "Do you think it was Josie?"

"It sounds so," Edna replied. "Martha said the girl worked in a bakery for a couple of months, but went into labor. She had her baby at the hospital."

"That verifies what we've put together so far."

"I have more," Edna said in her blunt way. "Martha said she saw the girl again just a few days ago. Said she looked frail and unwell. When Martha approached her, she turned and ran away."

"So she might be somewhere close still," Raesha said, her heart hurting for this frightened young girl.

"You should let Josiah know. He could go and search for her."

"Thank you, Edna. I appreciate the news. I'll tell Josiah."

Chapter Eight

Josiah pumped water from the old well so he could heat it over the fire and wash his hands and face. He and the other men had cleaned the well and got it pumping again. It would do for now. But he'd planned to install a pump inside the house and purchase a solar panel to help with heating water that could be pumped directly through the kitchen sink. He'd clear that with the bishop since some Old Order Amish frowned on such things.

This community seemed somewhere in between Old Order and the less conservative Amish. He only wanted a warm bath now and then and to be able to cook and wash clothes. But it would be a slow process. This morning, he was cleaning up scraps here and there since the house renovations were now finished. Soon, he could move in here with little Dinah.

That realization brought him both comfort and pain. He'd miss living at the Bawell place. But that arrangement could never be permanent.

Best to live here for a while and hope Josie would show up. If he had a stable home for the *bobbeli*, maybe his sister would be happy to join them and find some peace.

After he'd warmed the bucket of water over the fire he'd built earlier to burn wood scraps, he quickly washed up. He was about to go inside and admire the work his neighbors had done on the house and figure out if he wanted to build or buy some furniture to put inside.

"Josiah?"

He turned, surprised to see Raesha running across the tiny bridge between their property, her hands waving, her lightweight cape flying away from her shoulders.

He rushed toward her, afraid something had happened to Naomi. "What is it?"

Raesha stopped, her breath rushing out. "Edna Weiller called the shop. She's the midwife who visited Dinah. She had news regarding Josie."

His pulse quickened. "Is it bad?"

"*Neh*. At least, I think not. She has a friend who lives in Goldfield Orchard who saw a young girl, pregnant and staying at the Goldfield Bed-and-Breakfast. The girl went to a hospital to have her baby. But Martha, the friend, recently saw her again. She might still be in that area."

Josiah's heart stopped and then restarted with a rush. He whirled around and then turned back. *"Loss uns geh."* Let's go. "We must search for her."

"Do you want me to go with you?" she asked, surprise in her pretty eyes.

"I would appreciate that, *ja*." Then he stopped. "But...you'd be better help watching out for Dinah."

Her eyes filled with understanding. "You should clean up. You can call Mr. Craig to meet you at the Campton Center. He can go along with you and drive you to look for her."

She made good sense. He wanted to go right now but he was filthy. Looking down at his shirt and pants, he nodded. "I'll wash up and put on fresh clothing. I can clean up back at your place."

"I'll go on ahead. I need to get back to the shop. I'll check on Dinah and alert Mammi Naomi to what we've learned."

Nodding, he said, "I'll let you know when I'm leaving."

Raesha gave him a kind smile. "I pray you find her, Josiah."

"*Denke.* So do I."

After Raesha hurried away, Josiah stopped, took off his hat and looked out over the woods and fields. The sun shone brightly in a crisp midmorning glow. He closed his eyes and said a prayer.

"Your will, not mine."

But he prayed the Lord would show him favor.

Then he hurried to put away his tools and get to his buggy. He saw Raesha up ahead and caught up with her on the bridge. Her eyes met his and she offered a shaky smile.

"No matter what," she said, "you are a *gut* man, Josiah."

He wanted to be the kind of man who deserved a woman like her. He wanted to be a good uncle to Dinah and a good brother to Josie. He'd failed everyone in his family in so many ways.

Mostly, he wanted to find his sister and help her to turn her life back around.

The Lord had brought him here.

He'd wait on the Lord and then Josiah would set out to see that all of his wants became his reality. But the waiting would be so *hatt.* Hard. So very hard. Maybe that was the lesson the Lord wanted him to learn. Some things might be worth the wait.

* * *

Josiah pulled the buggy up to the Campton Center and hurried to secure the horses. Then he went inside to wait for Mr. Craig. Since he was staying nearby, he should arrive here quickly.

An assistant seated him inside Alisha Braxton's office. The attorney gave Josiah an encouraging smile. He brought her up-to-date, anxious while he fidgeted with the brim of his worn, faded hat.

"I'm still waiting on the birth certificate," he said. "I hope it will come through soon."

"It should have been there by now," Alisha said. "If you don't receive something in the next week, let me know and I'll try to track it for you."

Josiah thanked her and then waited.

"How did you meet Nathan?" she asked, her tone just below neutral.

"When I found out Josie had left Kentucky, I panicked. I had no idea where to start. A friend recommended him."

"But he lives in Pennsylvania. You were in Ohio."

"I heard he travels as needed. He was willing to go to Kentucky and ask around with me. And he's done some checking on his own now that I'm here."

That seemed to satisfy her. "I hope you find your sister, Mr. Fisher. It's tough when a loved one is out there alone and scared."

"*Ja*, she has been through so much."

Miss Braxton looked at her watch. "Just like Nathan to be late."

"Are you displeased with this man?" Josiah said, getting the feeling there was something amiss with this woman and the investigator.

Alisha tossed her thick hair back. "We don't always see eye to eye, but if I were searching for someone I loved, he'd be the only one I'd want to do the job."

"I'm reassured by that," Josiah said. "He has worked hard for me."

The front door of the big house creaked open and Nathan Craig walked in. Josiah stood and shook his hand. "Can we get going?"

Nathan's gaze moved from him to Miss Braxton. "I think we can. I know my way around Goldfield Orchard. I should have dug deeper last time I was there, but as you well know, the Amish can be tight-lipped about protecting one of their own."

Josiah bobbed his head. "I do know that. Makes it *hatt* to get anywhere sometimes."

"You two will make a good team," Miss Braxton said, her gaze touching on Nathan's.

"Now go. You have all afternoon but this might take longer."

"Wish us well," Nathan said.

"Always," she replied.

When her phone rang, she waved to them and went about her business.

"We'll make good time," Nathan said after they were in his sedan. "I won't drive fast, Mr. Fisher. Don't want to rattle you."

"I appreciate that," Josiah replied, feeling odd in this fancy roaring vehicle. "And you can stop calling me Mr. Fisher. Josiah is fine."

"All right, then," Nathan said with a rare grin.

Soon they were going over the details of all the clues they'd discovered in finding Josie. Nathan Craig seemed devoted to his job and he had the details down, from having Josiah describe her to a sketch artist to gathering every little morsel of information he could even if it didn't amount to anything.

"I'll track down that birth certificate copy for you, too," Nathan said.

"Why do you do this?" Josiah asked, wondering why the man seemed so committed.

Nathan watched the road and then said, "I was born Amish but I left during my *rumspringa* and never looked back. But I regret that at times. I had two brothers and a sister. She was the baby of the family. She went missing when she was twelve. We found her a few weeks later. Dead. And we never found her killer."

Josiah held to the dash, but glanced at his friend. "I am sorry, Nathan."

Nathan stared straight ahead. "I've made peace with it but I should have been there. I could have protected her."

"So this is why you help others search for their loved one, especially Amish who don't have the resources of most."

"Yes, no resources and no help. It's challenging but I know the life, know how difficult things can be at times."

"I will forever be grateful to you, Nathan."

"Don't thank me yet. I sure hope we find Josie."

"I pray so," Josiah said.

They rode in silence until they reached the quaint village of Goldfield Orchard. Josiah couldn't help but stare at every woman he saw, thinking it might be Josie. But he did not see his sister.

She'd probably stay out of sight or she might be working somewhere. Trying to make enough money to support her baby.

"Let's start at the bed-and-breakfast," Nathan said.

Josiah nodded in agreement, his stomach roiling with apprehension.

Father, please let me find her and make this up to her.

Naomi finished her work and grabbed Raesha by her sleeve. "Sit and eat. Dinah has been fed and changed. She is sleeping again. You are too worked up."

Raesha did as her mother-in-law asked. She sat down and stared at her food. "I have much to do in the shop. I think I should set up a little nursery there, too, so I can watch Dinah there at times."

"Are you concerned that I cannot watch the child?" Naomi asked, her tone gentle, her eyes keen.

"Neh," Raesha replied, her eyes full of love for Naomi. "You are gentle and loving but your balance is not what it used to be."

Naomi nodded at that. "We could both go tumbling down and I would not want that to happen."

"It's a concern," Raesha admitted. "I hope Josiah comes home with good news."

An hour later, she heard a knock on the back door.

Rushing to open it, she found Josiah standing there with his hat in his hands, his expression full of disappointment.

"You did not find her?"

"Neh."

"Kumm," she said, wanting to comfort him.

He slipped inside and glanced around. "I came for Dinah."

"She's sleeping," Raesha said. "Sleeping and full but it's about time for her to wake. If you're tired we can keep her with us awhile longer."

He smiled at her. "I'm tired and frustrated but she brings me comfort."

Raesha's heart felt a shard of pain. He only wanted to see the babe. Did he not see that she wanted to comfort him, too?

But that would be wrong. She could offer support and friendship and nothing more.

"Can I get you a bite to eat?"

He didn't argue with that.

Naomi came into the parlor and smiled at him. "Hello, Josiah. From the looks of you, I don't think you bring us good news."

"We searched everywhere," he said. Taking a place at the supper table, he shook his head. "Many had seen a woman matching her, but that was weeks ago. No one has seen her recently. They were kind in answering our questions but I think Josie has moved on."

"Keep searching," Naomi said. "She will feel your presence and, hopefully, she will feel God's love, too."

After he'd eaten a meat loaf sandwich and some mashed potatoes, Josiah turned to Raesha. "I can't thank you enough for helping me so."

"Dinah is a joy," she admitted, now holding the smiling child. "We love her dearly." Then she cooed at Dinah. "Don't we, sure we do."

The baby gurgled and kicked her little legs.

"I can rest knowing she is in *gut* hands. I owe you a great debt."

"You have helped out around here," Raesha pointed out. "Our machines are humming away without all the creaks and groans and my workers are impressed with your talents."

"Denke." He'd been disheartened when he'd come here tonight but now, as always, these two loving women had nurtured him with food and assurances.

Now he sat and watched Raesha holding his niece while he finished his meal. It hurt to see Josie and his *mamm* in Dinah's features. But seeing the way Raesha cared for her did bring him peace. What if Josie had left Dinah at another, less loving home?

He should be thankful for God's grace and

for Raesha's and Naomi's good hearts. Dinah was thriving here.

Raesha watched him and then said, "Josiah, I was thinking about setting up a place for Dinah in the shop, up front with me just behind the counter."

He stared from where she sat across from him, Dinah balanced on her lap, to where Naomi sat in her favorite rocking chair, mending clothes.

"Nowhere near the workroom," Naomi cautioned. "But Raesha is concerned with my old age and frail body and rightly so. I care about Dinah's safety so it might be best if she is with Raesha in the shop, where she will have plenty of able-bodied people to step up."

Josiah took it all in and then said, "I have a suggestion."

"What?" they both asked.

"Why don't we let Naomi be in charge of Dinah when one of us is around or nearby? She can hold her, feed her, rock her to sleep, and we can do our work within hearing range."

Naomi nodded at that, a deep appreciation in her eyes. "A *gut* plan."

Hopeful, he went on before Raesha could shut him down. "When I am working at the old place, Raesha will be in charge. Whether here or in the shop. I will help set up a baby area in the shop, wherever you want it."

She nodded. "Much appreciated. I will have lots of help. Susan comes from a big family. She is good with babies."

"And you have others who come and go," Naomi added. "This will be the most loved and cared for *bobbeli* in all of Campton Creek."

"How should we explain this?" Josiah asked, concerned that rumors would continue to fly. Used to people staring, he only smiled and nodded a greeting now. But he did not want these two women to bear the brunt of the rumors.

"We tell the truth as we have from the beginning," Naomi said without preamble. "We are helping our friend and neighbor with his little orphaned niece. That is all anyone needs to know."

"That is all," Josiah said, "but they will find out more and they will add to what they hear."

"We'll deal with that one day at a time," Raesha said. "We have to come up with a suitable and safe area for Dinah, and most have already heard that your sister is missing."

"I think so," he agreed. "I haven't offered much but people know and some have been kind. Others, not so much. But that is the way when we do not understand the situation."

Naomi watched them with her shrewd gaze.

"We will continue to help you, Josiah. Rest assured on that. We are learning as we go, however. It's been a long time since I held such a sweet little girl."

Raesha shook her head and smiled at Josiah. "So many details in raising a baby."

"That is true." He took a bite of his sandwich and washed it down with tea. "Josie gave her up for all the right reasons. She knew the child would be safe and loved here." Putting down his sandwich, he said, "I cannot imagine what she must have gone through. I knew she was troubled, but Josie would never give up a child without a *gut* reason."

"Now we hope we can find her and bring her here, too," Raesha said, her eyes holding his. "Wouldn't that be a joy?"

"It would," he admitted. "But what if she wants nothing to do with me…or her daughter?"

Standing, he stared down at Raesha. "If I never see my sister again, what will I tell that sweet little girl?"

Chapter Nine

The more he was around Raesha Bawell, the more Josiah realized she was different from any woman he'd ever known. In addition, she was smart, determined, faithful to a fault and outspoken on most subjects. Maybe this was what kept her single. Did most men scratch their heads and walk away?

He, however, found her candor refreshing. She wasn't disrespectful to anyone but she was firm and kind, with a no-nonsense attitude. He watched her now as she talked with the girl she'd introduced as Susan Raber. Susan held Dinah, her dark eyes bright with interest, while Raesha and Josiah moved an old bassinet they'd cleaned and polished into a cozy corner behind the long wide desk of the shop.

Dinah would be warm and safe here and away from the customers who would come and go. Even now, two Englisch women were admiring the *bobbeli*'s pretty eyes and bright smile. Susan handled them with expert ease, allowing them to look at Dinah but not touch her. Germs were everywhere. He did not want his niece to get sick.

"I'm ready to purchase my items," one woman said, her big coat flapping dangerously close to some trinkets on a nearby table.

"I can help you with that," Raesha replied, turning from where she'd placed a clean blanket into the bassinet. "We are sorry for the distractions today. But we have a little one to consider."

"She's adorable," the blonde woman said with a smile. "It's nice that she can be here with you while you work. You and your husband are truly blessed."

Raesha shot Josiah a glance while Susan's eyes popped wide.

"Denke," Josiah said. To explain more to a stranger would only make matters worse, but Raesha would have his hide since he didn't correct the woman.

The smiling lady glanced from Raesha back to him. "You two seem so perfect together."

Her tall friend gave her a stern warning glance. "Let's finish up here. We still want to tour the covered bridges."

Raesha rang up the shawl, gloves and candles, and then took the woman's money. Placing all of the items into a handmade bag with the shop's logo on it, Raesha thanked the customers and remained silent until the bell on the double doors chimed as they left.

Susan didn't waste a minute. "Are you two…?"

"No," Raesha said. "No, nothing is going on between us."

Josiah bobbed his head, suddenly too warm. "I did not correct the Englisch woman because then I'd have to explain the whole situation."

"You only had to say we are taking care of her for a friend," Raesha replied. "Or… I could have at least said that."

"Well, that's over now," Susan said to the smiling baby in her arms. "That woman will forget all about us when she sees our beautiful bridges. But if you ask me, I think these two do make a good match."

"Did little Dinah ask you anything?" Raesha asked, her eyes full of aggravation and mirth.

"No, not exactly," Susan retorted. "But she is a very wise young girl. She's smiling her agreement."

Josiah couldn't hide his own grin. Raesha's disapproving gaze moved to him. "And you were worried about rumors, so why are you trying not to laugh?"

Josiah couldn't explain it. "I don't know except that when you are all in a flutter you make me smile."

Susan giggled and then straightened her expression to look more somber.

Raesha turned back to spreading blankets and checking the bag of baby things she'd brought from the main house. "I am not all in a flutter. We will get adjusted to this but we don't need to give the impression we are more than friends. We have enough explaining to do as it is."

Josiah turned serious. "If this is too much for you, I can make other arrangements."

"Neh," Raesha and Susan said in unison.

"I like Dinah," Susan said. "I'll help out."

"I agreed to this," Raesha said. "There is no need to change our plans."

Josiah glanced from Raesha's stubborn face to Susan's watchful one. "Then I will return to my work. I'll come by later to pick her up."

"Pick her up? For what?" Raesha asked.

"To take her to the *grossdaddi haus* with me as usual."

"Oh." Raesha's eyes filled with acceptance and disappointment. "We did agree to that."

"*Ja*, and we've been doing that very thing for days now. Are you all right?"

"Of course. I just got busy and didn't know where you aimed to take her."

Susan's eyes went so wide, he was sure the girl was going to pop them right out of her head. "You're the person living in the *gross-daddi haus*?"

"*Ja*. I'm a paying customer and it was cleared with the bishop."

Susan glanced at Raesha. "This is so much better than chasing my brothers and sisters around."

"He's to take Dinah home with him at night, so they can get acquainted and he can learn how to take care of a *bobbeli*. Because he plans to sell his place and take her away to Ohio one day soon."

"Well, that's too bad," Susan replied, taking the now-sleeping Dinah to the fresh crib. "Because whether you two know it or not, things might not work out the way you've planned."

"What does that mean?" Raesha asked, her hands on her hips.

"That is between Dinah and me," Susan said on a giggle. Then she added, "God might have other plans for you two."

"When did you become so know-it-all?" Raesha asked with a mock tartness.

Josiah shook his head. Women and their riddles. A man could never guess what they truly were talking about. No wonder he was still single. He didn't know how to deal with all the emotions and unspoken expectations that came with women. He'd watched his *mamm* cower and give in to his forceful father, never knowing how she really felt. He had not learned the proper cues and warnings, or the proper courting tactics, with a woman.

But he'd spoken the truth earlier. Raesha made him laugh. She made him wonder. She made him happy. The kind of happy he hadn't felt in a long time. She didn't do many riddles but her bluntness was refreshing.

And yet she scared him. In that place in his heart, the place he'd boarded up and forgotten, she scared him.

"I must get to work," he said in way of an escape. "I will take Dinah this evening. I have her bed ready and I'll need you to show me how to wash diapers to get them…clean…again."

"That's my task," Raesha retorted, affronted.

"I'm willing to learn," he replied.

Susan seemed to be enjoying this too much. "I have never heard that said before."

Raesha nodded and straightened her *kapp* strings. "Very well. We will have a lesson in diaper cleaning and washing."

Josiah went out the side door to the yard, the crisp morning air bringing him relief. Inhaling deeply, he took off toward the old farmhouse, glad for something to take his mind off the woman who had somehow broken a seal inside his heart.

And yet, even in his angst and clumsiness, he couldn't help but smile. Maybe young Susan was right. Maybe he and Raesha could be a good match. But a lot would have to happen before that came to pass.

First being, the woman in question would have to show some interest in him.

Raesha knocked on Josiah's door, a plate filled with fried ham, two biscuits, and some rice and gravy in her hand. He had come to the shop to take Dinah for the night, but he didn't come over to the kitchen for dinner.

Not that she'd invited him or expected him. After Susan's pointed observations regarding both of them, she had decided to keep her distance from the man.

Then why was she standing here at his door?

When she heard Dinah crying, Raesha's heart leaped. She couldn't stop her need to protect the little girl. Josiah would take good care of her, but most men left childcare to their wives.

But you are not his wife.

The door swung open. He held a crying Dinah in a blanket, his face flushed and with worry in his eyes. "I'm not sure what's wrong with her."

Raesha stepped inside the cozy little house and put the food on the table. "Let me see."

Josiah gladly handed the babe to her. "I fed her and did a fairly *gut* job of changing her but now she's fussy."

Raesha shifted Dinah against her shoulder and started patting her tiny back. "Did you try to burp her?"

Josiah's confused stare was almost comical. "Burp her?"

"This," she said, still patting the baby. "You only need to gently pat her back so she can expel some air from her feeding."

Josiah watched silently as she calmed Dinah. "You seem so natural at this."

Raesha hummed a soft tune, one of her favorite hymns—"Precious Memories." She knew she had people praying her through the overwhelming events of the last week.

Father, I pray I do the right thing for all.

"You have calmed her," Josiah said, his hair mussed and his sleeves rolled up. "Clearly, I do not know what I'm doing."

Raesha's heart went out to him. He tried so

hard to please everyone. She wondered again what he must have gone through in the house across the way.

"If it becomes too much, we are here to help," she said. She wouldn't push him to let the child stay with Naomi and her all the time. He needed to learn how to be a good guardian to Dinah.

"*Ja*, and I am forever grateful for that."

"But you want to do your part?"

"I have to do my part. For Dinah, for Josie. But I have never raised a child. I want to do the best job I can. I had to take care of Josie after my parents died, but she was older and I had help in Ohio. This is different. Dinah needs constant care."

"I've not been blessed with children," she admitted. "Aaron and I wanted children and we thought…" She stopped, thinking this conversation had become inappropriate. "He blamed himself but…cancer took over our lives."

"I'm sorry for your loss," Josiah said. "But you seem to know what to do with children. I'm sure helping others has taught you to nurture."

She smiled at that and kept moving around the room until Dinah became groggy. "As we told you, we've housed a lot of people over the years. Family members who come and go, searching for something in their lives. Some come to visit and find their own homes here, some come for a few days or weeks and then go back home. Naomi came from a family of eight children, much like Susan."

"And you?"

"My parents have passed and my younger twin sisters, Emma and Becca, are both married and live right next to each other in another community about an hour or so from here. My older brother, Amos, also lives there but across the valley from them. When they come to visit, they usually stay for a few days. I get to spoil my three nieces and two nephews."

Josiah smiled at the sleeping baby. "This place seems to draw people in need. You and Naomi are kind and you have a successful business. I've dreamed of much the same. But I don't think it's in my future."

She listened and saw the anguish mixed with hope in his eyes. Taking Dinah back to her crib in the corner, she asked, "So you plan to go back to Ohio, *ja*?"

"I had planned to but now I don't know. If Josie is nearby, I need to stay close." Giving her a measured glance, he said, "I owe my *onkel* some money he loaned to me when I first went to search for Josie in Kentucky. One of my cousins is not happy about that and accused me of taking advantage of his *daed*."

After tucking the baby in, Raesha turned back to Josiah. "Ah, so that explains your need to sell out and go back to Ohio. You want to take care of things with your relatives."

"*Ja*, of course. I pay my debts."

"That is noble and shows you have integrity."

"Integrity but I need a steady income. I'm good with the land so I know I could make it here. I'm waiting to hear from Josie. She might show up back in Ohio or go back to Kentucky but I feel she's somewhere nearby."

The worrying about his sister had to be taking its toll on him. "I'm so sorry, Josiah. I can't imagine what you have been dealing with, searching for her, not knowing where she is or what might have happened to her."

"I know I should leave it to God but… I worry."

"That's a natural reaction, considering Josie could be alone and frightened."

He rubbed his eyes and nodded, his head down. "But God has sent us a gift, Raesha. Surely finding Dinah here is a sign to me, *ja*?"

Raesha couldn't speak. The agony in his words struck her to her core. "I believe so, Josiah." She couldn't ask him to stay simply because she loved little Dinah. That would be selfish and unkind. "You have to decide what is best for you and Dinah because you might not ever find your sister."

His head came up. "I won't stop looking. I can't. Josephine has suffered enough in her young life. I fear she got herself into some kind of trouble, based on how we were raised."

Raesha waited, hoping he would tell her.

But he turned away. "I've said too much. *Denke* for settling Dinah. I can take things from here."

"Eat your dinner while you can," Raesha replied, disappointed that he didn't want to talk about his childhood.

He nodded. "That and then I am going to sleep."

She went to the door but turned, her hand on the doorknob. "I pray you will find a restful sleep, Josiah."

He didn't speak. He stood staring over at her, his eyes dark with a whirl of emotions. Finally, he said, "The same to you."

Raesha went back to her side of the house and found Naomi sitting in her favorite chair by the warmth from the heater.

"Are you not ready for bed?" she asked.

Naomi patted the chair across from her. "I wanted to talk to you, daughter."

Raesha smiled. Naomi had called her daughter since the day Aaron had brought her here. "What is on your mind?"

"You and Josiah," Naomi replied, her hands folded in her lap. "That is what is on my mind, daughter."

Chapter Ten

Raesha's heart bumped. "What about Josiah and me, Mammi Naomi?"

Naomi slowly sipped her tea and took her time forming her words. "I've watched you two all week, with the *bobbeli*, with each other and even when you're not near each other."

"You don't have to worry," Raesha said, hoping to reassure her mother-in-law that Josiah was being a gentleman, proper and polite. "He's a kind man and he respects the boundaries that we abide by."

"I wasn't talking about propriety, Raesha," Naomi responded with a knowing smile. "I do not doubt you are beyond reproach."

Raesha shook her head. "Then what are you trying to tell me?"

Naomi shrugged her shoulders. "I think you two make a good match."

"What?" Raesha shifted in her chair. "Are you serious?"

"Very," Naomi said, her hands tucked against her lap shawl. "You need to find a *gut* man and I believe God has sent you one, and a babe to go with him."

Shocked, Raesha stood up and paced in front of the old propane heater. "It's a little too early to think such things, if at all, don't you think?"

"Never too early to find a soul mate." Naomi's kind eyes held hers. "But it will become too late one day."

Raesha had an image of herself, sitting in that very rocking chair, alone. Would anyone come to check on her?

Of course they would. She might be lonely but she'd never really be alone. Would she?

In her defense, she said, "But Josiah and I barely know each other and besides, he is determined to go back to Ohio to pay his *onkel* the money he loaned Josiah to search for Josie."

"That shows integrity," Naomi replied, as if she hadn't heard the rest of what Raesha had said. "But he can easily mail a check or some cash to his *onkel*. He might decide to stay here if he thinks you are interested."

Raesha sat back down on the chair across from Naomi. "I'm not interested."

Naomi didn't say a word. She was very

clever, knowing when to stay silent. It made others tell her everything on their heart. Raesha wouldn't fall for it.

But the silence in the big room and the quiet contentment in Naomi's expression made her twitch. "Okay, I might be interested."

"Just as I thought."

"But… I can't be interested. He has so much to do and he is concerned about Josie and Dinah. Josiah will do what's best for both of them. He put Josephine first when he took her to Ohio, thinking she'd be better off with family. But I wonder if his uncle and cousins treated him badly. He had no money and no hope when he left Campton Creek. He became indentured to them in a way, I believe. Now his guilt over all of it is eating away at him. He came back here to fix the place up and sell it, but I think he also came back here to put an end to the past and move on with his life. Only now, he has hope that Josie is still somewhere nearby."

Naomi's old rocker squeaked and creaked. "For someone who says she does not know this man, you sure seem to have learned a lot about him."

Wishing she'd stayed silent, Raesha gave Naomi a tight-lipped stare. "We've talked to each other, *ja*."

"Do you think he is interested in you?"

"No. I mean, I don't know. He could be but it can't come to pass."

"Why not?"

"I explained," Raesha said, thinking her mother-in-law could be very persistent at times. "He is going to sell out and leave and he'll take Dinah with him. End of story."

"And what about you?" Naomi asked. "Why are you holding back?"

"For one, I only just met the man a week ago, and you know I'm not interested in re-marrying."

"Aaron would want you to do just that. You can still love and mourn my son, but you could also honor him and be happy in this life, too."

Naomi tried to stand and Raesha rushed to help her. "I am fine in this life. I am blessed and busy with work I love. I'm content."

Content. There was that word again. Raesha had never doubted that contentment and happiness went hand in hand. But now she doubted what true happiness really meant.

"I think this is the beginning of a new story," Naomi said with her serene smile intact. "Give it some time. You have to admit finding the babe and the *onkel* in one week has to be God's doing."

"Yes, but I don't think God wants me to rush

his doings," Raesha said, her words calm while her mind raced with embarrassment and annoyance. Josiah was a handsome man with his broad shoulders and dark curly hair. How could she not notice him? He filled any room he came into, especially her kitchen.

But why did everyone think she needed to be married to be happy? She'd been content...

Raesha stopped short, a new realization causing Naomi to glance over at her. Yes, she'd been content. But happy went deeper than content.

She could see that now and she felt that difference each time she looked at Dinah or saw Josiah walking across the footbridge between their homes.

"We will let nature take its course," Naomi said, her tone soft, her smile full of assurance.

Raesha turned back Naomi's bed and then gave her a kiss on the cheek. "*Gut* idea."

Naomi wasn't finished. "But remember, do not let me stand in the way."

"You are not in the way," Raesha replied, love pouring over her heart. "This is between Josiah and me and... God will show all of us the way."

She wouldn't leave Naomi alone no matter that any number of people would gladly move in here with her mother-in-law or take Naomi in. Raesha couldn't bring herself to leave. She'd built a life here and she loved the Bawell property, the hat shop, her workers, her friends and this community.

"*Denke*, for caring about me," she told Naomi. "Now you need to rest."

She helped Naomi into her nightgown and gave her the pills the doctor wanted her to take each night, and together they said their nightly prayers, which now included praying for Josiah, Josephine and little Dinah.

Naomi finished the prayer. *"Im Namen des Vater, des Sohns, und des Heiligen Geistes."*

In the name of the Father, the Son and the Holy Ghost.

"Amen," Raesha said in unison with Naomi.

Then she turned down the lamp, tucked the blankets tight and left the door slightly open. She'd listen in for Naomi while she finished up some knitting and mending in the parlor. Because she knew sleep would not come to her right away.

She couldn't stop thinking about what Naomi had suggested earlier and she couldn't stop thinking about the man and the baby so nearby and yet so out of her reach.

September moved with the swiftness of a reckless wind toward winter. The woods had changed to a more barren landscape and the trees were beginning to shed their various leaves. Snow would come soon, and with it the busy Christmas season at the shop.

For now, Raesha and Josiah settled into a daily routine where he brought Dinah over early each morning and Raesha and Naomi watched her during the day while he worked on the old place next door. Raesha took Dinah to the shop with her on most days, but Susan had become so efficient, Raesha had begun to go in later and come home earlier.

"I don't mind," Susan kept insisting. "I love my work here and I'm helping support my family. Besides, you need time with the little one away from all the fuss here in the shop. We're all right here, doing our jobs, like clockwork."

Of course, Susan got to see Daniel a lot more at the shop, too. It seemed to be a winning situation for all and Raesha expected to be making another wedding bonnet soon.

But she gave another young girl who lived around the curve some extra hours to help Susan.

"I'll figure something out before we get too busy," she'd promised Susan.

Raesha had to admit she enjoyed seeing Josiah every day, too, and on the occasional night when he needed help learning how to handle a baby. But she tried not to show how

Josiah made her heart leap or that her head got all befuddled.

Naomi watched them together with unabashed pleasure and Susan kept her keen eyes on them whenever Josiah came into the shop to check on Dinah. The employees had gotten to know him and appreciate him. Especially when he would lend a hand here and there, always inquisitive about hat-making.

Then he'd come back to pick Dinah up just as the sun was slipping away over the tree line. Somewhere in there over the last couple of weeks, he began staying for dinner, rather than taking a plate to the house he rented.

Probably because Naomi had said one rainy night, "Why don't you just eat here, Josiah? It's the practical thing to do."

Naomi was all about being practical.

Raesha couldn't protest. That would be disrespecting her elder. And what would it hurt to have Josiah share a hearty meal with them while they all spoiled Dinah? It saved her having to walk it over since he couldn't carry a plate of food and Dinah and all her supplies, too.

She had to admire the way he'd taken to his niece. Most men would frown on such hands-on helping with childcare. But Josiah had experienced taking care of his young sister. He didn't seem to mind middle-of-the-night feedings and changing diapers.

Raesha washed most of the baby clothes and hung them to dry even if he insisted on washing his own clothes, and he'd given his best to scalding and bleaching diapers, too.

A stubborn, proud man who didn't want to seek help from anyone.

A knock at the door brought Raesha out of her musings. Some friends were gathering here this afternoon for a frolic—quilting, baking and making plans for the fall festival that would take place in town near the Hartford General Store. Campton Creek held a spring mud sale and a craft festival each year and managed to squeeze in a couple of fall and harvest festivals and, sometimes, mud sales before winter set in.

Susan grinned when Raesha opened the door. "I brought apple fritters and oatmeal cookies from Mamm. She let me escape!"

"I'm so glad to see you," Raesha said, tugging her inside the warm house.

"As if you didn't just see me earlier at the shop," Susan replied, glancing around. "Where is my wee friend?"

"Dinah is sleeping," Raesha replied with a finger to her lips. "And so is Naomi."

"*Gut* to have an afternoon off," Susan mock-whispered. "Wednesday is always a slow day for the front."

"While the back of the shop is steady with work," Raesha replied. "Daniel is getting very good at being the boss back there."

"He loves his work," Susan said with a soft smile. "And he appreciates that you trust him."

Susan went about helping her set out refreshments: coffee, lemonade and tea, along with fruit and nibbles. Then her young friend whirled to stare at Raesha.

"Do I have a bug on my nose?" Raesha asked, waiting patiently for Susan to spit out whatever was going through her always-bubbling head.

"Was it hard for you to take over the business? I mean, as a woman?"

Raesha put down the folded yellow cloth napkins she'd taken out of the cupboard. *"Ja,"* she admitted with a sigh. "The men who work in the hat shop were used to taking orders from Aaron and his *daddi* before him. At first, they refused to even acknowledge me. I had to keep smiling and giving out orders."

"When did they come to respect you the way they do now?" Susan asked, her eyes wide with curiosity.

Raesha thought about it. "Ah, that happened a few months after Aaron had died. I needed a rush order for a client two counties over. They were lollygagging about and I came into the shop and stood with my hands on my hips."

"You were perturbed?"

"Slightly." Raesha smiled now, but she remembered how her heart trembled that day. "I told the foreman to shut down the machines and then I announced that the Bawell Hat Shop was my world, because it had been my husband's world. I told them I now had to take care of Naomi—that sweet old woman who had no one else to help her. I didn't want to let her down and I reminded them of all she'd done for them, too."

Susan burst out laughing. "You shamed those young men."

"I did and I'm not ashamed to admit that. Slackers are not welcome in my shop."

"You know, Raesha, we all admire your spunk."

"Who is *we all*?"

"My friends and I, Mamm, everyone I know. They respect Naomi and admire you for staying by her side. Is that why you've not married again?"

Shocked at that question, Raesha shook her head. "I am fine with my work and my home. I fell in love with Aaron and I also fell in love with this place. I could never leave it for anyone."

Susan's impressed smile changed when she looked past Raesha to the now-open side door.

Raesha turned to find Josiah standing there with a confused, disappointed expression on his face.

Had he heard her declaration?

Chapter Eleven

Josiah couldn't get Raesha's words out of his head.

She'd never leave her home. Her words had burned through him hot as a branding iron. *He'd* left his home without even bothering to rebuild it. Up and left it gutted and charred and abandoned, thinking he'd had no other choice. After the horrible fire and his parents' deaths, he'd only wanted to get as far away from the farm as possible.

Why hadn't he waited and let the community help him rebuild way back then? If he had, Josie might be happily married by now and living at the old place with her husband. Or he might have found a wife here and could have made a life working the land.

At the time, he wanted his sister to never have to see that house again. And he did not want to have to explain to everyone how the fire had happened either. Had he been wrong to guard so many family secrets?

Now he regretted his hasty decision to uproot Josie and start over fresh somewhere else. But at eighteen, he hadn't known what to do or where to go. His mother's people had long ago moved on and most had died. His father hated his family and talked badly about them, but Ohio had seemed the only place left for Josiah and his traumatized little sister. Even though they had not been welcomed with open arms, his *onkel* had taken them in. Only to work both of them so hard, Josie rebelled and took off.

But something else about Raesha's words had grabbed at him.

She'd never leave this community. Now as he worked on the old barn, tearing away vines and weeds, knocking down charred boards and broken windows, he had to admit it had crossed his mind a time or two that she would make a good wife.

But would she follow someone like him?

Would she give up her life here to go to Ohio?

No. He had to quit thinking that way. She was firmly settled and had a thriving business, something unusual for a widowed Amish woman. She was good at her work and good with little Dinah. What if she wanted both? Her work and a family?

Could he handle that?

He'd been handling that.

Raesha's work ethic impressed him. He'd been inside the back of the shop and watched how Daniel King and her other workers took extra care to create handmade products. Raesha and Daniel had guided him on steaming brims and measuring felt to match the patterns and the sturdy paper hat forms. He'd seen the women sewing away on treadle machines, their hands moving the materials to make the stitches perfect. Daniel and Susan had told him all about straw suppliers and how to wet the straw and weight it down with bricks or rocks to shape it.

So many sizes and shapes. He'd worn hats all of his life and had never given a thought to how they were made. For a brief moment, he thought he could be content learning that trade.

But he didn't know if he'd stay here.

Father, I need to turn this over to You. I need to focus on what needs to be done now.

A lot still needed to be taken care of with this farm. The Fisher farm covered only a few acres but they'd managed to eke out a living here. Or so he'd always believed. His mother, Sarah, had somehow made money on the side to help feed her family. Until Abram Fisher had discovered she'd been hiding money from him.

Josiah stopped, took a breath, inhaling over and over. The memories of the fire always disturbed him even though he'd been away at the time. But Josie remembered what she could and had mentioned details at the oddest moments. What must those same memories have done to her? She'd been only nine and she'd witnessed the whole thing. He feared those memories had driven her to destruction.

She'd had a child. Josie wouldn't give away her own child unless she'd had no other choice. Obviously, she had not married Tobias, the boy she always spoke about in her letters.

Telling himself he wouldn't leave until he got word from the lawyer lady or Mr. Craig regarding Josie's whereabouts, Josiah felt caught between a rock and a hard place. Stay here and hope his sister would return home? Or go back to Ohio and bear the brunt of his cousin's wrath and his *onkel*'s grudging kindness?

As hard as this work was, here was the best place right now and maybe for the rest of his life.

But where would that leave Raesha and him?
There is no Raesha and you, he told himself. *She has everything she needs right here. And you have nothing to offer her.*

He stopped hammering at the old wood and turned to stare over at the Bawell place. The two-storied house shone a clean white against the October sunshine. A warm spell had hit and the temperatures were crisp but pleasant. The house seemed to glow against the golden-and-russet leaves of the trees. The big barn stood solid and tall behind the house. The mums lining the porch welcomed people to the big door and the fall garden grew hardy and bright.

Then he looked back around at his place. Forlorn and torn, half-broken and withered, half built back to new. He'd had only half a life here anyway and not a very good life after he'd left.

Left his mother and sister without anyone to defend them. Would he ever get over the guilt of that, so he could finish rebuilding his life?

I have failed, Father. I don't know how to make it all right again.

He wasn't good enough for the likes of Raesha Bawell.

He'd never been good enough for his father or his extended family and he'd failed his sister miserably.

Deciding he'd get this place ready to sell as he'd planned, Josiah accepted that if he couldn't find Josie, he might have to move on. But where? Did he go back to Ohio to stay?

Or did he find another community and start all over again?

Father, what am I to do?

His life seemed so overwhelming at times. How many walls would he have to tear down to find peace and contentment?

Josiah went back to his solitary work, his thoughts and prayers on how to find true redemption. He'd have that only when he knew Josie was safe.

Much later, he heard a buggy approaching and turned to squint into the late afternoon sun. Jeremiah Weaver waved to him and hopped down to hurry toward him.

"*Gut* day, Jeremiah," Josiah said, nodding. He and Jeremiah had met at the general store and gotten to know each other when Jeremiah had come to help Josiah with rebuilding the house. Jeremiah had been a prodigal who'd returned to his faith and was now happily married and had a baby boy to add to his new wife's two older children.

"Morning, Josiah," Jeremiah said, glancing around. "You've made progress here."

Josiah dusted off his hands. "*Ja*, but more is needed."

Jeremiah nodded and stared out toward the woods. "Listen, I was doing some work at the

Campton Center and…a phone call came in for you."

"For me?" Josiah put down his tools. "Who would be calling for me?"

"Alisha Braxton got a call on your behalf. It's about your sister, Josiah. Mr. Craig has located her. But she's sick and in a hospital about thirty minutes away."

Shock coursed through Josiah. Josie! Dropping his toolbox, he said, "I must get to her."

"Kumm," Jeremiah said, his blues eyes full of urgency. "I can take you to the Campton Center. We have a driver there who volunteers to taxi Amish as needed."

"Denke," Josiah said. Then he looked toward the Bawell place. "I have to tend to Dinah."

"I'm sure the Bawell women will take care of her."

"I'll tell them I have to go," he said, his mind full of questions. "Josie needs me."

Jeremiah touched his arm. "I'll drive you over to get whatever you might need."

Together, they headed to the waiting buggy.

Josiah couldn't speak. Josie was alive but ill. He had to get to her right away.

This could change everything and very quickly at that.

What if Josie wanted nothing to do with him?

* * *

Raesha waved to the last of her friends, her mood upbeat in spite of their teasing her about the new developments in her life. She couldn't let their pointed suggestions sway her in any way.

"I've heard he's handsome," Deborah Troyer said with a knowing smile. "And available."

"I saw him in town," Beth Weaver added. "Jeremiah said if he's rebuilding the old place, he might consider sticking around?"

"He plans to sell it." She tried to explain. Several times.

But the women were off and running on a thread of speculation that moved as quickly as their nimble fingers against patterns.

Beth went on. "He can't take care of sweet Dinah alone. He's blessed that you are being so kind, Raesha."

Deborah smiled over at the crib. "Dinah is such a good *bobbeli*. She needs a mother."

Another friend added, "Yes, Raesha, she needs a mother."

"Time will tell what Josiah decides," Naomi said in her best commanding voice. "Until then, enough. We are here to work, not to make idle assumptions."

She sent Raesha a serene smile and then winked at her.

That shut everyone down on that subject. The women moved on to children and housework and what they planned on bringing to the Campton Creek Fall Festival next weekend. They quilted and mended and crocheted and knitted, the tightness of their teasing, well-meaning love as strong as the threads they wove.

But Raesha had seen the sweet concern behind the comments. They wanted her to have a family of her own.

Tired now and still smiling about their comments, Raesha turned to go and check on Dinah when the back door burst open and Josiah stood there, his expression full of shock, his eyes wide.

"What's wrong?" she asked, her heart jumping with dread.

"They've found Josie," he said, his hands on her arms. "I must go to her."

Josie. "Where, how?" Emotion crashed through her in great waves. She didn't even mind that he'd grabbed her arms.

He named the hospital toward the west. "Jeremiah came to tell me. There is a taxi waiting at the Campton Center."

"Go," she said. "Go to your sister. Dinah will be fine with us until you return."

"I don't know how long I'll be gone."

Seeing the struggle in his eyes, Raesha held his gaze. "Go to your sister, Josiah. I promise Dinah will be taken care of until…" Stopping, she inhaled a breath. "Until you bring her *mamm* home."

His eyes filled with gratitude and surprise. "If I can bring her home. You do not mind? She can stay with me in the old house. It's put together enough—we'll move over there and make do."

No, they wouldn't make do. The house needed furniture and lamps and heat, not to mention a new stove and all sorts of other things. Raesha knew she wouldn't send them away. Especially not with little Dinah. She couldn't be sure if Josie would be able to take care of her own child.

"We will discuss that later," she replied. "Right now, go and see what is wrong with her. And stay as long as you need to do so."

He held her arms and then realized what he was doing. Dropping his hands away, he kept staring at her. "You are a kind woman, Raesha."

"Your sister will need a lot of time and quiet to recover. We have the room available. And Josiah, we will pray for you to bring her back and soon."

He nodded and whirled to hurry to the *grossdaddi haus*.

Raesha watched him go inside and then turned and held her hand to her heart.

What if Josie wanted her baby back? What would happen then?

Chapter Twelve

Josiah walked up the long hospital hallway, the sound of machines beeping and voices calling urgently overhead jarring him. Somewhere a phone rang. A nurse answered it, her tone calm and professional. Then in another room, a well-dressed woman wept while she held a sleeping man's hand.

All of this was foreign to him but the kind nurse at the big desk had told him he'd find his sister in room 102.

"At the end of the hallway."

Josiah stopped when he saw Josie's full name on the sign by the door. *Deidre Josephine Fisher.*

Their father had not approved of the names. He'd wanted his daughter to have a more humble name. But she became Josie and that seemed to fit.

Taking a breath, Josiah pushed at the door and silently peeked inside. Josie lay sleeping, her dark hair long and thick but not as shiny as it once was. Her skin, always pale, now looked washed-out and she had dark circles underneath her eyes.

When a doctor came toward him, Josiah glanced around.

"Could I have a word with you, Mr. Fisher?" the young doctor asked, his voice low.

Josiah looked at his sister again and then came back out into the hallway. The doctor motioned to two chairs by a large window with a view of fall across the hills and mountains.

"I'm Dr. Caldwell. Your sister has been through a lot."

Josiah glanced to the partially opened door. "She ran away and I couldn't find her. But I had reason to believe she was nearby." He didn't plan on mentioning the baby.

"She's very sick," the doctor replied. "She had pneumonia and honestly, if she hadn't come to us when she did, I don't think she would have made it."

Josiah absorbed that information and then asked, "How did you find her?"

"We didn't," Dr. Caldwell replied. "She stumbled into the ER about four days ago. She's been in ICU and we just now moved her to a private room. She was so sick and she was hallucinating."

"How so?" Josiah asked, knowing what that word meant.

"She kept talking about her baby."

Josiah closed his eyes and felt a pain so deep, it took his breath away. "She had a child," he finally said. "I now have the child, a baby girl, with me."

The doctor nodded. "We discovered that she'd given birth from examining her but we couldn't be sure when. So you knew?"

"Not until recently," Josiah said. "I came back here to search for my sister and take care of some property. She had left the baby with my neighbors."

"How long ago was that?"

"A couple of weeks now," he admitted. "After hiring an investigator, I learned the child was related to me. She will grow up Amish."

The young doctor glanced around and then said, "Your sister won't be able to leave the hospital for a few more days and then she'll need a safe, comfortable place to rest and recover. Can you provide that?"

Josiah nodded. "*Ja*, I have kind neighbors who are helping me with the child and they have offered to let Josie stay with them, too.

Two widowed women who are experienced in fostering."

The doctor nodded, seemingly satisfied. "When you go in to see her, don't ask a lot of questions," he suggested. "She's not only physically frail but…whatever happened with her has left her shaken and frightened. She might not be ready to talk about it."

Josiah nodded and then asked, "So has she mentioned a husband?"

"Your sister told us she is single," Dr. Caldwell said, standing to check his pager. "But she did ask for you. She asked for her brother and told us she thought you were in Campton Creek. We called the Campton Center, hoping someone would find you. A man named Nathan Craig verified you were in the area."

"He has been searching for her," Josiah explained. "And now, I have found her. *Denke*, Dr. Caldwell."

Josiah watched the doctor hurry to his next patient. But he had to wonder—how did Josie know he was back in Pennsylvania?

Josiah went back into the room and sat down beside his sleeping sister. He took Josie's hand, noticing how skinny it felt inside his bigger one. Her skin seemed to droop around her. She'd always been healthy before, robust and all girl. Now she'd become a shell of herself.

Josie moaned in her sleep, her head moving as if she were denying something. How he wanted to take away all of her pain.

She let out a soft cry and then opened her eyes wide.

"Josiah?"

He heard the plea in his name.

"I'm here, Josie. I'm here," he said, his hand squeezing hers. "It will be all right now."

A single tear fell down her face and she looked away, out the window toward the hills. "It's fall."

"*Ja*, did you not remember?"

"I don't remember a lot of things," she admitted.

Then she went back to sleep.

Josiah held her hand, his head down while he prayed. Not knowing what to pray for, he only asked God to guide him. He had to take her home and nurture her and watch over her. He wouldn't let her out of his sight this time.

He had other concerns now, however.

His sister had a baby out of wedlock and then left that baby abandoned on a porch.

Would the Campton Creek Amish community accept her with open arms or would they shun her and make her life hard to bear?

He knew his people back in Ohio wouldn't want her there.

But what about the people here? They had once belonged to the Campton Creek community. He'd have to clear all of this with the bishop, of course. Josie would have to confess before the church and turn her life back over to God.

Was that why she'd come back here? Was that why she'd called out for him? Would the community shun her?

So many questions. If she couldn't live among the Amish here, he'd have no choice but to take her away. Again.

So he prayed and sat with her, talking gently about all he'd done to the house and how kind the neighbors had been, until the nurses came in and told him he'd have to leave. The sun was setting over the trees and hills.

"I'll come back tomorrow," he said to her, over and over. "I won't leave you again."

Giving her a gentle kiss on the forehead, Josiah turned to the nurse. "You will let me know if anything happens, if she has a change?"

"Yes. I promise." She took the number to the hat shop, smiling and nodding her head. "I'm familiar with the Bawell shop. Such a nice place. I shop there for Christmas and birthdays a lot."

"I'm renting from them," he explained. "I can be reached through that number and the one at the Campton Center."

"We'll put that information in her charts," the nurse replied. "Go home and rest, same as your sister. She needs that more than anything else right now."

"Will she be all right?" he asked as they walked to the door together.

"In time, I hope," the nurse said. "In God's own time."

Josiah left with a heavy heart and found a taxi outside to take him home. The thirty-minute drive seemed like a lifetime.

After the driver dropped him off, he stood outside the Bawell place and stared over at the home he'd left. It looked better now, thanks to the help he'd received from this giving community. But the new facade couldn't hide the pain his family had suffered inside that house.

Would that be the best place for Josie right now?

Before he could form a thought on that issue, the front door of the Bawell house opened and Raesha came hurrying toward him.

"Josiah, you're back."

He walked to meet her by an ancient oak tree in the front yard. "*Ja.* They wouldn't let me stay. Said she needs her rest."

"Will she be all right?"

Seeing the concern in Raesha's pretty eyes almost undid him. "With time, the nurse said." Then he told Raesha what the doctor had reported.

"Pneumonia. That's serious," Raesha replied. "I'm thankful she went for help." She glanced into his eyes. "She must have been so afraid. God's grace has brought her back to you."

He nodded. "The nurse told me she was in a homeless shelter, freezing and sick. One of the volunteers there is a nurse and she told Josie she needed to go to the hospital. Josie refused but then sometime in the night, she left the shelter and found her way to the hospital down the street. Collapsed inside the emergency room doors."

"Oh, my." Raesha held her arms against her stomach. "Have you had supper?"

"Neh." He'd forgotten to eat and he wasn't sure he could do so now either.

She took his elbow. *"Kumm*, Josiah. You need nourishment and you can visit with Dinah. She's awake."

Exhausted, Josiah followed her inside and took off his hat.

"You can wash up. We have pot roast, rolls, and carrots and peas."

Suddenly, he was starving. *"Denke*, Raesha."

Naomi came out of the bedroom, holding Dinah close. "She has been changed and bathed. I'll put her in her little crib and she can sit with us during supper."

He saw the glance that passed between the two women but tried not to speculate on what it meant. After washing his hands and running water over his face at the sink, Josiah dried his hands and rolled the crib close.

"She looks so much like her mother."

Naomi motioned for him to sit across from her and Raesha. "Tell us about Josephine."

And so he did. In between bites of the delicious roast with potatoes and buttered rolls, he described his beautiful little sister, comparing the way she looked today with the way he remembered her. "She deserves better than this," he said. "She deserves some happiness."

Raesha shot a glance to her mother-in-law again.

"You do not want her here?" he asked, dropping his fork.

Naomi shook her head. "No, no. You misunderstand our concern."

"And what is your concern?"

Raesha sipped her hot tea. "We wonder if she'll be capable of taking care of Dinah."

"Ah." Now he understood, a sweet relief washing over him followed by a deep concern.

"I don't know the answer to that question yet. She is weak in body and spirit, according to the doctor. He advised me not to pester her with questions. She slept while I talked, but I did not mention the *bobbeli*. Will it be a problem if she doesn't take to Dinah right away?"

"No," they said in unison.

"No," Raesha repeated. "We only want both of you to know that we are here and we will help however you need us."

Satisfied, he nodded. But then, he'd seen a shard of relief in Raesha's eyes, too. Did she want Josie to be a real mother to Dinah or was she afraid Josie would take the child away?

Finishing his meal, Josiah took the fresh coffee Naomi brought to him. "I'll have to go back and forth to the hospital until she's better," he said. "I think it might be best if Dinah stays here in the house with you until I can bring Josie home." Then he added, "And maybe even after."

"We'd be happy to have her," Raesha said, smiling at Josiah's wide-eyed expression.

Josiah decided Raesha would be happy to have his niece for a very long time to come. Was he right in letting her spend so much time with a child whom she might not be able to keep with her?

But what other choice did he have? He

trusted Raesha with Dinah and until he knew how Josie would react to the baby, he couldn't ask for a more perfect substitute mother.

Then something hit him in the gut, making his stomach roil. He couldn't imagine any other woman in his life either.

But how could he even think about these new feelings now, when his life was in such an uproar?

"You must be so tired," Naomi said. "Would you care for some apple pie?"

Josiah looked up to find the older woman smiling at him. Did she know he'd just been hit with a lightning bolt of shock?

"I'd enjoy that, Mammi Naomi," he said, his gaze shifting to Raesha.

"Gut," Naomi replied. "Raesha will be glad to slice you a piece. I'm tired myself. I think I'll go on to my room."

Raesha and Josiah looked at each other. The expression on her face showed the same fear and awe that went swirling through his stomach. Would he be able to eat pie?

"She rarely goes to bed this early," Raesha said after handing him a slice of cinnamon-infused apples inside a flaky crust. "But this has been a trying day."

"You don't want to be alone with me."

His statement brought her head up. "Why wouldn't I want to be alone with you?"

"It's not proper?"

"We have two very capable chaperones—my mother-in-law and your niece. One refuses attention and the other one needs it constantly. I don't think we'll be alone at all."

"*Gut* point."

They both burst out into giggles.

"Shh," Raesha said, her grin glowing. "She can hear very well for her age."

"Which one?"

More giggles and then somber expressions as they studied each other. Really studied each other.

"Your pie is growing cold," she finally said, dropping her head.

"So it is." He ate in silence, the day's events caving in on him. "Do you worry that bringing Josie here will cause concern in the community?"

"We will not turn her away."

"But…she is not well and…something happened to her. Something that I fear to even voice."

"We will help her heal. She will be left alone but surrounded with love. I promise you that, Josiah."

"What if she is shunned?"

"We'll consult the bishop. I pray there will not be a ban put on her, and I hope he'll understand she needs shelter now and she needs to heal."

"Don't we all?"

Raesha lifted her head, her eyes on him. "Will you tell me one day?"

"Tell you what?"

"About what really happened in your house? What caused that fire?"

Did she know the truth?

"What do you mean? Have you heard something?"

"No. But I wonder. Josie was a young girl and she watched her parents perish in a horrible way. That has to change a person."

"It did," he finally said. "But I don't know what happened, exactly. She only told me she was playing outside and saw the fire."

"Your parents were there?"

"In the house." He took a breath, hating to even think about that horrible day. "She said that she ran in to tell my folks and they both hurried to the barn. That's the last time she saw them. She never talks about it beyond that."

Raesha nodded and got up to remove their dishes. "This place has a way of opening up our hearts to reveal all of our secrets. I think Josie needs that kind of healing now."

"Will you be all right if she wants Dinah back?" he asked, needing to know.

She placed the plates in the sink basin but she didn't turn around. "Why do you ask that?"

He came close but refrained from forcing her to look at him. "I can see how much you adore my little niece. And I thank God each day that Josie left Dinah with you. But I worry that you'll become too attached to Dinah."

She whirled then, her eyes bright with a mist of fear and resolve. "I'm already attached to Dinah," she admitted. "But I know that God's will has to be accepted, no matter my pain."

Staring out the kitchen window, she said, "I had to watch my strong, proud husband die and I accepted that. I had to learn to run a business on my own, in spite of the odds, and I accepted that. I think I can handle it if Dinah has to leave us…but it will take a while to get her sweet presence out of my heart."

Josiah didn't move. "What if you didn't have to let her go?"

Pivoting back to face him, she asked, "What does that mean?"

"What if you and I—"

Dinah let out a wail, causing them both to jump.

"I'll attend to her," Raesha said. Then she glanced at him over her shoulder. "Go and get some rest, Josiah. You'll want to get back to the hospital early in the morning. Your sister needs you."

He'd been dismissed. He'd misread her.

She didn't really want *him* in her life. But she did want Dinah.

He left, his heart heavy with worry and wondering.

What would Raesha have said if he'd finished his question?

Chapter Thirteen

The next morning Raesha went into the shop early. The Harvest Festival would be held the third week of October and she had several tasks to complete before a stream of tourists arrived at her place of business.

"Daniel," she said, calling into the back where the quiet would last only a few more minutes, "did we get that shipment out to New York?"

"Yes, Mrs. Bawell," Daniel replied, his smile soft and full of respect. "All loaded and boxed and Ben delivered one hundred winter hats to the shipping store. We left the receipts in your box on the desk."

"That's a relief." She checked the long shelves lining the wall inside the organized shop. "We have a fair amount of inventory in both summer and winter hats. I think we're on schedule."

She'd been concerned since her life had changed so drastically in the last few weeks. A baby and a handsome renter, and related to each other at that. Feast or famine around here.

Lord, You do challenge me but I'm thankful for the opportunity.

Her life had been less than challenging lately. Almost stagnant and too still. She'd become complacent. Not anymore.

Nodding in approval to Daniel, she said, "What would I do without you?"

Daniel shrugged. "You know I love working here. Considering I've been doing it for two years now, I hope you know you can depend on me for anything."

Trying not to read too much in her young friend's declarations, Raesha knew the whole community must be abuzz with the happenings in the Bawell house.

"You are kind," she replied. "Things have changed in my life, for the good I think, and I am grateful that you were able to step up and keep the shop running smoothly for me."

"My job," the young man replied, his smile beaming. "I'll get the festival booth set up out front. Susan and I will man it and we have people scheduled to help."

"Susan and you." Raesha watched him blush.

"She is a *gut* girl, Daniel. I'm happy for both of you."

He looked so confused, she almost laughed. Maybe he didn't realize he was in love. "You do care for Susan, *ja*?"

Gulping in air, he bobbed his head. "*Ja*, but I didn't think anyone noticed, especially her."

"Oh, trust me, she has noticed," Raesha replied. "I can vouch for that."

The man grinned from ear to ear.

Raesha went through the mail, laying aside anything that wasn't urgent. Then she saw an official-looking envelope from the country records office. The birth certificate?

When the back door to the shop opened, Raesha expected to see another employee. But Josiah walked in and gave her a nod.

"Excuse me, Daniel," she said, hurrying away.

Daniel's eyes held amusement mixed with questions.

Maybe her workers *had* noticed something between her and Josiah, too. She needed to be careful in how she acted around him. While they'd done nothing inappropriate, rumors could still fly. The man had enough to deal with already.

"Josiah, I think this is the document you've been waiting on."

"The birth certificate?" He took the envelope and tore it open. Then he nodded his head. "Deidre Josephine Fisher—*Mudder*. Baby girl—Dinah Charlotte Fisher. Born on July 18 of this year." He shook his head. "She loved that book, *Charlotte's Web*." Looking back at the paper, he said, "No one listed as the father."

"Then that is final proof," Raesha said. "Josie is truly your niece."

"I already knew it, but yes, this is official proof."

He stood for a moment, his head down.

"Did you need me?" Raesha asked, thinking that was a loaded question. "You came in here for something?"

"I only wanted to let you know I'm leaving for the hospital. I saw Dinah and helped feed her a morning bottle. I thank you for calling your friend to come and be with Naomi and her."

"Beth Weaver loves babies," Raesha said, thinking what woman didn't. "You know Jeremiah is her brother."

"Yes. He's been a comfort to me."

"He was a prodigal but he is home and fully committed to Ava Jane and their children now. His best friend, Jacob, was her first husband. She already had a boy and girl when Jeremiah came back into her life."

"There is hope," Josiah said, his always-tumultuous gaze moving over her face. "I didn't sleep very well, but I pray that my sister did."

"Go and be with her." Raesha heard doors opening and people chattering. "My staff is arriving for the day. I have to go over some of the things we need to get done before the Harvest Festival."

"I'd forgotten that is approaching. Maybe I can do more if Josie is feeling better."

"Do not think about it," Raesha replied. "You've done enough by helping with our ornery machines in the shop and fixing our rickety booth for out front."

"I've always been handy with contraptions," he admitted. "I had to learn a lot on my own, growing up."

Raesha saw a shadow fall across his face. He went dark each time he mentioned his childhood. She wished he'd talk to her but only when he felt sure enough to do so. Letting it go for now, she watched him leave and hurried about her business.

But she couldn't deny what that birth certificate had proved. Dinah belonged to his sister.

She prayed his sister would be able to talk to him when he got to the hospital and that the girl would turn out to be a mother to her child.

* * *

"She had a rough night," Nurse Ruthie told him in a whisper. "She's frightened and physically weak. Maybe you can get her to eat some pudding and broth."

"I'll do my best," he said. "Josie can be stubborn."

"So we've noticed. But that stubbornness is what made her seek help. She wants to live."

"I hope so," Josiah replied. "I want her well."

Nurse Ruthie guided him into the quiet room. "Josiah, she might need some counseling once she's better. Someone to talk to about her fears and emotions."

He understood what the nurse was saying. "The lawyer lady suggested that, too. I will seek that help at the Campton Center."

"A great place to start," the nurse agreed. "Judy Campton and her volunteers have great resources and they come without a bill to pay."

Josiah wondered about his sister's hospital bill but he'd deal with that later.

When they went inside, Josie was sitting up but staring out the window. The sunny day should brighten her mood, even if the view couldn't.

"Hello, Josie," he said.

She didn't even look around.

"I see you didn't prefer your oatmeal," Nurse

Ruthie said. "Josie, you need to eat to gain your strength. Would you allow your brother to help you try a bite or two?"

Josie turned her head, her gaze catching Josiah. The fear and shame in her expression broke him. She shook her head but didn't speak.

The nurse took the tray and left the room, shutting the door behind her.

Josiah took off his hat and pulled a chair up close to the bed. "How are you today?"

His sister's big eyes widened. "Why are you here?"

"Because I love you and want to bring you home. They said you asked for me."

"I don't remember asking for you. I can't go home. That part of my life is over."

"I'm staying near the old place," he said, careful not to upset her. "If you'd like, we could live there again."

She twisted away, a hand going to her heart. "You left me there before."

Josiah lowered his head, her cold words burning through him. "I did and I regret that."

"I don't know where I should be."

"You should be with me. I won't leave you again."

Josie stared down at her hands. "I can't go back to Kentucky."

"Would you want to one day?"

She shook her head, tears forming in her eyes. "I can't, Josiah. I just can't."

Then she slid down and pulled the covers up. "I'm tired."

"You should rest. I'll be here when you wake up."

Josie watched him with somber eyes. "Why did you come back here?"

Glad she was asking, he nodded. "I heard you might be back in Campton Creek. I've been searching for you since…since I got word that you had left Kentucky."

Josie closed her eyes. "You should leave me alone and get back to your life."

"You are a part of my life. I shouldn't have let you go to Kentucky."

Her eyes opened wide. "Why do you say that?"

"Because you ran away and—"

He stopped, unable to say the words.

"And had a child," she finally said, each word a whisper. "You know, don't you?"

Josiah didn't say anything at first. Then he gazed at her, his heart bursting with agony. "Josie, you left her on my neighbor's doorstep. Did you hope I'd find her there?"

His sister clammed up and turned away. "I don't want to talk about that."

Josiah stayed with her another hour while she

moved in and out of sleep. The nurses and doctors made their rounds, checking her vitals and encouraging her to eat and rest. He watched as they forced her to take breathing treatments to keep her pneumonia from coming back.

"She needs to get up and move about," Nurse Ruthie told him. "She's weak but exercise will give her strength."

He needed to get back to work, but before he left, he touched his sister's arm, knowing she wasn't really asleep.

"Josie, will you let me help you take a short walk in the hallway?"

"I don't feel like it."

"If you don't move around, you could become ill again."

"I'm better."

"*Kumm* now. One turn up the hall and back and then I must get back to Campton Creek."

She lifted her head to stare at him. "You should have stayed away. I had a plan and you messed it up."

"Was that plan to leave your child with strangers and never let me know?"

She bobbed her head, looking every bit the humiliated little sister he remembered. "She is better off with them."

He lifted Josie up and coaxed her to stand.

She wobbled and he held her. "Why do you think that?"

"You know why."

"No, I don't. I do not know what happened to you."

He had her up. But when he offered her a robe she shook her head. "I'm not going to walk with you. Because you want information and I have none to give."

Pulling away, she turned back to the bed and almost fell. Josiah helped her back in and covered her. "Tomorrow, we walk. Be ready."

"You don't need to come every day."

"And what will you do when they release you? You can't stay here forever."

"I'll go back to the shelter."

"You will not."

"You sound a lot like *Daed*, you know."

That statement, said with such malice, floored Josiah.

"I am not my father, Josie."

"I hope not," she retorted. "I'll figure this out, Josiah. The way I always have."

He wanted to remind her of where that had gotten her but she looked exhausted and, as the nurse had told him, his sister was fragile. So he touched a hand to her arm and then turned and left the room.

This would be a big battle. His sister had always had a mind of her own. He'd tried to bear the brunt of their father's wrath but Josie saw it and had to have heard it. At times, she ran from the fights to hide away in the barn.

Now the past surrounded them in bitter memories.

Did he try to keep her here, with those memories?

Or should he take her away to try to help her heal?

He couldn't leave Campton Creek right now. Josie would have to accept staying with the Bawells for a while.

But he wouldn't break that news to her until the doctors released her and she had no other choice.

Raesha took the clothes off the line and carried them inside, the clean scents of sunshine and fresh air surrounding the sheets and towels. She placed little bags of dried lavender in the linen cabinet that stood in the big upstairs hallway. It made the sheets smell as fresh as a garden.

Taking a set of sheets to the *grossdaddi haus*, she opened the unlocked door and went inside. Josiah kept the place clean. No dust anywhere and no dirty dishes in the sink. The man was so self-sufficient she could hardly believe her eyes.

He was a bachelor but he didn't act like one. But then, he'd mentioned having to learn things on his own growing up.

Did his father not teach him about life?

Again, she had to wonder what he and his sister had suffered. For years, she'd glanced over at the old place but the trees between the properties had kept most of it hidden from her. When she came out of the little house behind her home, she took a deep breath and decided she'd go for a walk after she put away the rest of the sheets and towels. Just over to the Fisher farm. Maybe if she stared up at the house long enough, she'd find some answers.

When she came through the back door, Naomi stood to meet her. "We have a visitor," her mother-in-law said, giving Raesha a pointed warning glance.

Raesha looked past Naomi to find her sister Emma standing there. "Emma, is everything all right? Is someone sick?"

Her sister, so young and vibrant, smiled and shook her head. "*Neh*, silly. Can't I take some time to *kumm* and visit my older sister?"

"Yes, but where is Becca? You two always come together." The better to gang up on her.

Emma's gaze moved around the room and

landed with such accuracy on the crib in the corner that Raesha immediately understood. Her sister had come snooping.

"Where is Becca?" Raesha asked again, her gaze moving from Naomi back to Emma.

Naomi remained as cool as a cucumber, her smile gentle, her eyes piercing with subtle warnings.

"Becca has two sick *kinder*," Emma said, her green eyes bright with questions. "What's going on with you, Raesha?"

"What have you heard?" Raesha asked, cutting the chatter. "Because I know you didn't drive all this way just to be chatty."

Emma shrugged. "Well, since we live near Goldfield Orchard, word got out that the hatmaker in Campton Creek had found a baby on her porch. Then we heard two men had come asking about a missing Amish girl who'd been seen in our area."

"So you put two and two together and decided to come and check on me?"

Emma held her hands over her white apron. "David brought me, *ja*. We took a taxi into town and then borrowed a horse and buggy from David's cousin to ride over here."

David's cousin lived away from town in a small isolated house to the west. He wouldn't have known much about the happenings in Raesha's life since he ignored most people anyway.

So she couldn't blame him. Word had traveled and her curious, concerned sisters would want answers. So here stood Emma, lovely and fresh faced, a happy mother come to see if her older sister was up to mischief or doing good.

Or rather, she'd talked her loving husband *into* bringing her, Raesha decided. Well, it was inevitable. She'd been so preoccupied she'd neglected to head this off at the pass.

Since she had not done anything wrong, she stiffened her spine and smiled. "What would you like to know, Emma? I'll give you a thorough report so you can explain all the details to Becca and Amos."

Raesha suspected her brother would be curious and furious. He tended to control the family, of course.

Emma moved farther into the room and then stopped at the crib. "A little girl?"

Naomi made a face and shrugged. "She knows this already. Your sister has a way of pulling the truth out of a person."

Emma grinned. "But Mammi Naomi has a way of not really answering any questions."

Raesha joined Emma, her gaze moving to the crib, where Dinah slept. "So now that you are here, it is *gut* to see you."

Emma hugged Raesha tight. "We were only worried about you."

"I understand and appreciate that," Raesha said, holding no ill will.

"I couldn't help it," Emma said. "When people started talking, I knew I had to come and check on you. David took Sara and Lara to see the covered bridge so we could visit. I hope you don't mind if we stay overnight."

"Of course not. You must have a lot of questions," Raesha replied. Then she tugged her sister close again. "You know you are always *wilkum* here."

Emma smiled and said, "I'd love to hold her when she wakes up."

Raesha's eyes got misty. Her sister loved her and had come to see if she was all right. But the family would want the truth.

"I should have contacted you sooner," she admitted. "Josiah, this little one's *onkel*, was the one asking about the missing girl. The man with him is an Englisch private investigator."

"Josiah, is it?" Emma replied, her hands on her hips. "Why don't you start with him?"

Chapter Fourteen

Josiah knocked on the back door, weary from seeing his sister so despondent and sick. But he needed to give Raesha a break and he figured holding little Dinah close would make him feel better.

When Raesha opened the door, her expression held apprehension and concern. "Josiah, you're here early today."

He stood as usual with his hat in his hand. "I came straight from the hospital. I'll take Dinah with me for the rest of the day."

Raesha cast a glance over her shoulder, her actions full of hesitation. "That would be fine. Can you come inside for a while? She's awake now and…we have company."

Wondering what was going on, Josiah stepped inside to find a petite young woman holding Dinah but staring up at him.

"I'm sorry," he said. "I can come back later."

Raesha looked from the woman back to him, trepidation in her eyes.

"Josiah, this is my sister Emma. Her twin is Becca and I have an older brother—Amos. Emma lives in Williamson Way, which is near Goldfield Orchard, but she and her husband have come to visit."

Suddenly, Josiah understood. Raesha's sister must have heard something. She might even remember seeing Josie. He wanted to ask but stopped himself.

Instead, he nodded and smiled. "It is nice to meet you, Emma."

The woman stared at him, assessing him with bright green eyes. "It is *gut* to meet you, too, Mr. Fisher. My sister had been telling me all about this new development in her life."

"That would be my niece and me," he admitted. "Raesha and Mammi Naomi have been kind to me." His gaze touched on Raesha, who stood solid and tall, her chin up and her gaze on Dinah. "I will never forget their generosity."

Raesha's eyes lifted to his with a sweetness that took his breath away.

But Emma's eyes widened. "Dinah is a sweetheart. I can understand why my sister is so smitten…with her."

Josiah heard the little gasp Raesha tried to

hide. "I can come back later since you two are visiting," he offered, nervousness overtaking him.

He'd never been good at conversation and especially conversation with a woman. Besides, her sister was eyeing him with way too much interest. Would he pass the test she obviously wanted to give him? Did she think he'd take advantage of the young Widow Bawell? Never? Or had he already?

Confusion made him break out in a sweat.

"So you live on the property?" Emma asked while she swayed back and forth, smiling down at Dinah.

"I've told you—he lives in the *grossdaddi haus*," Raesha said, shooting her sister a daring glare.

"I wanted to be sure I understand," Emma replied. "I'm surprised the bishop allowed that."

"The bishop approved it because I'm here," Naomi said with a slight lift of her voice. "I make a fine chaperone and nanny."

"I wasn't implying anything was wrong," Emma said, looking just a little chagrined. "But... I have to consider my sister."

Raesha motioned Josiah out of the spot where he stood frozen. "Sit down at least. I'll get you some spice cake and tea."

Emma placed herself at the table, too, her

smile light and her mood chatty. "Spice cake and tea sounds great. I'll have some, too, while I get to know Josiah."

He looked up at Raesha, wanting to shout for help. But he wouldn't be a coward. "What would you like to know?"

Emma's smile never wavered. "So you once lived next door? I suppose you'd already moved on and never even knew Raesha when she married Aaron and moved here."

"I left when I was eighteen," he replied, the memories of taking Josie away tearing through him.

"And went to Ohio, I hear."

"Ja."

"And now you're back because your sister went missing and you have realized Dinah is her child, but you're also here to sell the farm next door. Then you'll take off again?"

Josiah glanced at Raesha. "I…uh…"

Raesha hurried over and set a plate full of chunky cuts of spice cake on the table. "Eat your snack, Emma. Because you can't ask questions with your mouth full."

Her sister chuckled and held tight to Dinah. "Okay, I know I'm being nosy. I'll hush now."

"You know about as much as anyone," Naomi said, shaking her head. "And maybe more than most."

Josiah and Raesha both looked at her but she only smiled and reached for her own slice of cake. "What a nice time we'll have at supper tonight. We have much to catch up on, don't we, Emma?"

Emma's amused gaze swept the room. "We do at that. David should be along soon with the *kinder*. They will love seeing a baby in the house."

Josiah saw a flash of hurt passing through Raesha's eyes. He wanted to tell her well-meaning sister to form her words more carefully. She meant no harm and yet he could almost see the bit of smugness in her words. Why did everyone think a woman had to be married with children and that she should not go against her husband at all?

His own mother had tried to please his *daed* over and over. Until the bitter end. They'd died together trapped in that barn.

Or maybe only one of them had been trapped. Maybe the other one had wanted to die there. But not alone.

"I must go," he said, getting up so fast he almost knocked over his tea glass. "I'll come back to get Dinah later."

Raesha sent her sister a warning glance and walked him to the door, a perplexed expression on her face. "Will you take supper with us?"

Josiah didn't think he was up to any more questions. "*Neh.* I just want my niece with me tonight. I'll make myself a sandwich at home."

She looked disappointed but didn't press. "I'll see you in a little while, then."

Josiah nodded and slapped his hat on his head. He had some thinking to do. He'd felt this way before, torn and hurting and wondering what to do. But those times had involved Josie and what might be best for her, or trying to please his strict uncle and resentful cousins.

These feelings rushing through him now were new and different. He cared about Raesha and wished he could do something nice for her, to show her.

But that would be wrong on his part. He'd already taken up too much of her time, and each day she grew closer to Dinah.

Torn between wanting to make Raesha happy but wanting to help his sister heal so she could raise her own child, Josiah started walking. He kept walking until he came upon the big covered bridge that spanned the deepest part of the creek.

The bridge seemed to be holding this community together, a strong backbone that supported anything that put weight on its sturdy cross-beamed structure. The bright red of the wood had faded to a mellow pinkish patina, worn in places and rich in other places. Life. This was a place that followed life while the creek flowed and moved and filled up during floods and went shallow in dry times. The gurgle of the water below only highlighted his thoughts and brought him a measure of peace and relief. Who could predict life anyway? He'd tried to live a good life, but he'd failed over and over.

He couldn't dream about a woman who had everything except the one thing she longed for and she couldn't leave her happy life here to follow a vagabond such as him around the country, searching, always searching, for his own happy ending.

Gott, am I not worthy of a happy life? Could You show me how to be a better man so I can work on my flaws?

Maybe this bridge would be a good spot to ask the Lord for help. Josiah stood there, watching the creek flow, seeing fish jumping here and there. A hawk flew over, curious. Some squirrels frolicked in the trees along the shore. Birds chirped and fluttered. Life continued, no matter the currents hidden underneath the surface.

He heard laughter and turned to find a beautiful woman walking toward him, two older children by her side. She held a dark-haired baby in her arms. They looked so perfect, it pained him. Would he ever have a family of his own?

When the woman drew close, she smiled and waved. "Hello."

The boy ran ahead and nodded to Josiah. The girl glanced at the water and back to him. "Can you swim?" she asked.

"Sarah Rose, what a question to ask," her mother admonished. "Can you at least say hello?"

"Hello," the pretty girl said. Then she ran toward her brother.

The woman shook her head and shifted the giggling baby onto her shoulder. "She learned to swim two years ago, after she almost drowned right down there. We are thankful but now she wants everyone to know how to stay safe around the water."

"I'm so sorry," Josiah replied. Then it hit him. "You're Jeremiah's wife, *ja*?"

"I am," she said, her blue eyes bright. "Ava Jane Weaver. I see you've heard that story. He saved Sarah Rose's life and now he's a part of our lives." Then she looked Josiah over. "And I'm thinking you're Josiah Fisher. My husband goes on and on about you. He considers you a new friend."

"That's me," he said, taking off his hat. "Jeremiah has been a *gut* friend to me."

She beamed with pride. "He has a way with people. Maybe because he's been on the other side of life out there. He's more dedicated to his life here than ever before. But it took us a while to find our way back to each other."

"I can see he's happy," Josiah said, his tone wistful.

"But you are struggling?"

"In so many ways. I won't bother you with my problems."

"Nonsense," she said. "Why don't you walk home with us and stay for supper."

"I...uh... I don't know." He had Dinah to consider.

"You look like you need a friend," she pointed out.

Josiah did need a friend. Someone who wasn't so pretty she made his eyes hurt or so kind she made him want to be around her all the time or so funny he couldn't stop laughing. He needed a friend who could listen, just listen, and then give him a knock on his noggin and tell him to do what he had to do, not what he wanted to do.

"I'd appreciate having supper with you and your family, Mrs. Weaver," he said.

"Call me Ava Jane," she replied. "Now I have to corral those two before they go looking for tadpoles."

She called to the two older children. "Eli, Sarah Rose, hurry along. We have a guest coming for dinner."

The *kinder* rushed up and surrounded Josiah, asking him rapid-fire questions. He started laughing while he tried to answer.

"See, you're feeling better already," Ava Jane said.

When they came to the yard, Jeremiah turned from drawing water at the well and waved. "What have we here?"

"We found him on the bridge," Sarah Rose explained with her hands on her hips. "I think he's staying for supper."

Jeremiah laughed. "Then I'd better finish washing up."

As they approached, he reached for his son, his eyes on his wife. "I see you've met JJ and his *mamm*."

Josiah nodded. "You said you were a blessed man. Now I can attest to that. You have a wonderful family."

"I do," Jeremiah replied. "I do." Then he clapped Josiah on the back. "And did I tell you she's a great cook at that?"

* * *

"Raesha, why are you so restless?" Emma asked after they'd cleared the supper dishes. "Are you worried he won't come for the *bobbeli*?"

Raesha glanced to where David sat with their twin girls, talking quietly with Naomi while she rocked Dinah.

"He'll be here soon. He's usually not this late. Most nights he has supper—"

"Here with you," Emma finished, her expression knowing.

"Here with Naomi and me," she replied, tired of trying to cover. But she had done nothing wrong. "Not every night."

"But a lot of nights," Emma said.

"Okay, most nights."

"This is about more than helping a friend, isn't it?" her sister asked.

"Why would you say that?"

"I see the way he looks at you, sister," Emma replied. "And I see the way you look at him. Do you have feelings for this man?"

"I like him," Raesha admitted. "He is a *gut* man."

"That may be so but he comes with a lot of baggage."

"I can't believe you said that," Raesha replied. "He's had a hard time of it most of his life. He's trying to raise his little niece and he just found his sister. She almost died and she has a long way to go in healing properly, in both body and spirit."

"I'm sorry for all of that," Emma said. "I have to worry for you, though."

"I will be fine. I'm always fine."

"*Neh*, you are not. You weren't fine when you had to watch your husband die a horrible death."

"Are you trying to help me or make me feel worse?" Raesha asked, her voice raised enough to make David and Naomi glance up.

"I'm trying to figure out what you expect from this man. Do you plan to be his nanny for the rest of his time here? Or do you want more?"

Raesha couldn't tell her sister she wanted more. So much more. What could she say?

A knock at the back door brought her up and out of her chair. "That must be Josiah now."

"Saved by the knock," her sister teased. "But this conversation isn't over."

"I figured as much," Raesha said with a twisted smile.

But it was over for now. She wasn't ready to share her feelings with anyone, not even herself. Right now, she only wanted to help Josiah take care of Dinah and accept that the child might not be with her always. The baby belonged to another woman, a troubled, fragile woman. Josie could recover and demand her child back. Then they would all probably disappear right out of her life just as quickly as they'd come into her life.

But how could she watch them go now that they were embedded in her heart?

She opened the door, her emotions boiling over, her soul pierced with a dull ache that she so wanted to fix.

Josiah stood there, his dark eyes holding hers. "I'm sorry I'm late. I had supper with Jeremiah and his family."

Something in his words touched her. "You needed to get away from all of this, right?"

He nodded. "I had a lot on my mind."

"I never asked you how Josie was doing today."

"Not so *gut*," he admitted. "I'm worried for her."

He glanced into the room. Emma had joined her family with Naomi. His gaze fell on Dinah. "I can see that my niece is safe and being spoiled."

"It's hard for anyone to resist her sweet smile," Raesha said. "Do you want to come in and meet David and the twins?"

"Your sister, a twin, has her own twins, too?"

"She does. God has a sense of humor, I do believe."

They laughed together, easing the tension.

Then he came farther into the room. "Before I meet them, I wanted to ask you a favor."

"What is that?"

Leaning in, he said, "Would you mind going with me to see Josie? I thought if she had a woman to talk with, she might respond better."

Surprised, Raesha wasn't sure what to say. She glanced back at her family and then looked up at him.

"You don't want to do this?"

"It's not that, Josiah," she said. "I'm just wondering how she'll react to the woman she left her baby with coming to visit her, how that might make her feel."

"I think you could bring her comfort and reassure her," he replied. "And maybe that will help her to decide to come home."

Raesha's heart pulsed with pain. Did she have the courage to help this troubled young girl? The girl who had the power to break her heart if she took her baby back?

"I will be glad to talk to Josie," she said, knowing she had no other choice. "I'll make arrangements to go with you to visit her as soon as my sister leaves tomorrow."

"*Denke*, Raesha," he said. "Now let me meet your brother-in-law and those pretty little twins."

Chapter Fifteen

The next afternoon, Raesha hugged her sister goodbye. "*Denke* for coming to check on me. Will you give a good report?"

They'd enjoyed supper last night and after her sister had spent some time with Josiah, Emma seemed better assured. Josiah had a way of conversing with ease even if he did seem so shy at times.

Emma grimaced and then nodded. "I'll tell the truth. You are helping a neighbor. It's not as if you and Naomi haven't done this before. You took Becca and me in for a while, hoping to make a match for us, remember?"

"How could I forget?" Raesha replied. "Neither of you liked our choices. But you went on to find wonderful husbands on your own."

Emma's smile said it all. "Ja, and even though I should pay you back by messing in your business, I am not going to do that. This is too personal and too close to your heart, ain't so?"

Tears pricked Raesha's eyes. "It is too much, too soon. I have much praying to do. I read my Bible and wait for answers but… I have to abide by the will of the Lord."

"I think the Lord's hand is all over this one," Emma said, her gaze gentle. "He has placed a wonderful man and a sweet baby right in your hands. But I will keep your secrets close, sister. You know, though, Becca will want details and Amos will be all gruff and demanding. I'll stand firm and tell them you are fine and you are doing what you do best—helping another human being."

Relieved, Raesha held Emma's hands in hers. "I can only pray you don't cave and blurt out everything. Because I'm not so sure what the truth is right now. My heart is all mixed-up."

"I still don't know your true feelings either," Emma admitted. "But I'm pretty sure everyone else who sees you two together has it figured out."

Raesha slapped at her hand. "No one has anything figured out. We're all just spluttering along, trying to find our way."

"Emma?"

They turned to find David waiting with the buggy. "We have to go. Now."

"I'm coming," she called. Turning back to Raesha, she said, "We don't want to miss our taxi home."

Raesha hugged her sister again. "Love to all. I wish you could stay for visiting Sunday."

"I have to get back," Emma replied, waving as she hurried to the buggy. "Becca will be frantic and frazzled. I'm sure she'll need help with the *kinder.* I hope they are all feeling better now."

"So do I," Raesha said. "Give them one of those snickerdoodles we made this morning."

"If I can keep David and my twins from eating all of them."

She waved them away and then turned back to go inside, but stopped in the yard to take a look across the way. Toward Josiah's place.

The house looked fresh and new, rebuilt and painted a clean white with stark black shutters. It wasn't a large house. Built on the four-square model from what she'd heard, with the small front porch added later. But it seemed to be sturdy again. She wondered if the man rebuilding the house was also trying to rebuild himself and his faith, piece by piece.

Isn't that what we have to do, Father? I pray You will help all of us rebuild, especially Josie.

Raesha had tried to readjust her attitude toward the wayward girl who'd left a baby at her door. She did not know what Josie had been through, but who was she to judge?

So she'd prayed a lot, read the Scriptures and consulted Naomi while they were alone after Emma and David took a walk with the girls earlier.

"You are wise to pray about this," Naomi said, understanding in her eyes. "It's difficult, either way."

"He wants me to visit her. I told him I would but I can't see how I'll help."

"She needs a woman's counsel."

"But me? I have her child in my home."

"She made the choice to leave the child here."

"What if she gets angry, or worse, goes all silent on me?"

"We keep trying," Naomi said. "Shunning is one thing and we will deal with that if it happens. But forgiveness is always the best first step to finding true peace. For you, this means you have to accept that this girl has suffered some sort of trauma and she had good reason to leave her child in a safe place."

"I also have to keep telling myself that no matter what, Dinah is not mine to keep. I might have to let her go, whether she lives next door or in another community far away from me."

Naomi took her hand. "I'm praying about

this situation as always. The Lord will show us the way."

"*Gott*'s will."

"It is the only way to accept things we have no control over."

Now as she gathered her things to make the trip to the hospital with Josiah, Raesha steeled herself against what might come. Glancing toward the shop, she missed the days when she had gotten up, had breakfast with Naomi, then walked to the shop door to get down to business. While she'd never worked full days since she had responsibilities in the house and in the fields, too, she still loved the energy of being in the shop, helping customers and talking to always-curious tourists.

She felt as if she were neglecting the very business that had kept her going. Busying herself with work kept her mind off losing Aaron and not having a family of her own.

That constant, steady routine had been shattered and shifted but in a way that also brought her a new kind of happiness. And the worst kind of pain.

I will get through today, she told herself. Then she'd bring in reinforcements to set up the tents in front of the shop so they could show off their wares during the festival next week. She and her staff had everything in order—the quilts, knickknacks, pillows, shawls, artwork and hats, of course. Along with baked goods and jams and jellies. They always had a large booth with plenty to display.

That she could deal with.

Her task today would be difficult.

But when she turned and saw Josiah coming toward the back door, she knew she had to be doing the right thing. He looked so lost and forlorn, her heart beat harder for him.

"I will do my best, Father."

She only prayed her best would be good enough to help Josiah and his sister.

"I appreciate you doing this," Josiah said as they headed to the Campton Center to catch the taxi they'd reserved. "You are busy with the shop and the festival...and helping me. I will find a way to return the favor."

"You've already done enough," she reminded him. "Fixing up the creaks in the house and putting new hinges on the squeaky doors makes my life easier."

"Creaks and hinges, my specialty," he teased. "I'm also *gut* with a hammer and nails and with tearing out old boards. I have the cuts and bruises to prove it."

She laughed at that. The weather today was clear with a crisp chill. Early fall weather. Tugging her lightweight black cloak closer, she took in the fresh air. "When will you have your barn building?"

"I don't know," he said. "Samuel suggested after the festival. More manpower then."

"I will plan out the meal schedule," she said, already seeing it in her head. "We can line up tables near your property and I'll have the women bring food for dinner. You'll all be hungry and we'll all get to visit."

"You take on anything, don't you?"

"I take on what needs to be done, *ja.*"

"I've never known a woman like you."

She glanced over at him, trying to gauge if that had been a compliment or a complaint. Maybe a little of both.

"What kind of woman am I?" she asked, needing to know.

Josiah sent her a quick glance. "The truth?"

"I want to hear the truth."

"You are kind, loving, encouraging and you work hard."

"I think I can live with those descriptions."

Clicking the reins, he added, "This might be too forward but you are also very pretty."

She blushed and tugged her cloak close. "I am plain and simple but that's a nice compliment."

He looked at her in full then, his eyes holding hers. "You will never be plain and simple, Raesha. You have a sweet soul."

"Denke." She had to look away. The man had a way of making her feel all warm and cold at the same time. "Is it my turn to compliment and critique you?"

Lowering his head, he said, "What do you think of me?"

She watched the road, seeing other Amish buggies passing and checking when a vehicle honked at them, afraid of what he might find in her eyes. "You are a *gut* man who is trying to do his best. You work hard for yourself and anyone in need. You want to do right by others even when it's uncomfortable or not in your best interest."

"You have me figured out, I see."

His tone indicated disappointment. "Does that upset you?"

"No. You got it right. But… I've changed so much in the last few weeks. I realize I've made mistakes that I might not be able to repair."

"God's grace will sustain you, Josiah."

"I'm leaning on that." Then he gave her another quick glance. "Do you find me…appealing?"

Raesha knew they were stepping into dangerous territory. "You are a nice-looking man."

"Nice looking?" He grinned and tugged at

his hat. "I would hate to turn your face sour each time you look at me."

"You do not turn my face sour," she said on a giggle. "Seems when I'm with you, I laugh more than I normally do."

"And that's what I admire about you. You make me laugh and you laugh with me. It is *gut*, ja?"

"It is *gut*," she replied. "But we have much between us that we cannot laugh about."

"I will try to remedy that."

They arrived at the Campton Center and after he had secured Chester in a fenced area with water and food, they found the waiting taxi. Soon they were on their way to the hospital.

Sitting in the back seat next to Josiah in the comfort of the fast-zooming automobile only made Raesha more aware of the man. This morning, he smelled clean and fresh, like the air around them. His dark, shiny hair was combed but still untamed. It curled and flipped around his collar and ears. His clothes were clean and tidy.

Touching her *kapp*, she thought of how she'd been so careful in picking her own clothes today. A maroon dress pinned with a clean white apron, dark hose and sturdy walking shoes. Her hair secured in a bun beneath her *kapp*.

She'd dressed to look nice for Josie, to show

the girl that she meant no harm. But she'd also dressed to make Josiah proud, to look special in his eyes.

Am I wrong, Lord, to think such thoughts? Am I following Your will or trying to bend things toward my own way?

When they reached the hospital and entered through the busy, sterile main lobby, Raesha held her breath and prayed for guidance and clarity.

She was afraid of what she might find.

She was afraid the woman lying in that hospital bed had the power to break her heart. And so did the man who'd asked her to come here.

Josiah knocked softly and then pushed at the partially open door, then entered Josie's hospital room. The room was quiet and dark, the bed empty. At first he was afraid Josie wasn't inside.

His sister was sitting in a chair by the window. When she heard the door open, she turned to look up but she didn't smile or acknowledge him. She wore a pink robe, her dark hair braided down her back.

"Hallo," he said, wishing he could find his sister somewhere underneath that shell. "How are you today?"

"I'm okay," she said. "One of the nurses

brought me a robe." Then she looked beyond him, her eyes widening in fear at the sight of an Amish woman standing in the doorway. "Who is this?"

Josiah tugged Raesha into the room. "This is Raesha Bawell. The woman who is caring for your daughter."

Josie gulped a breath and put a hand to her mouth. "Why did you bring her here?"

Josiah now wished he hadn't asked Raesha to come with him today and that he hadn't blurted that out. Nervous and unsure, he couldn't bring himself to speak. He didn't want to upset his sister but she needed to see that she would have a peaceful place to stay when she came home. And that her baby was safe and well.

Raesha pushed past him and slowly sat down in a chair across from Josie. "I insisted he bring me here. I wanted to let you know that Dinah is healthy and thriving and that we are so blessed that you chose us to take care of your baby. She will be loved and cared for until you feel up to taking her back. I promise you that."

Josie's eyes boiled over with tears. She gripped the arms of the chair, her knuckles turning white, and began to shake her head. "*Neh*, I can't take her back. You must understand, I cannot raise her. I do not want to be with her. I left her with you for a reason."

Raesha lifted her gaze to Josiah, shock in her expression. "Why don't you want her back?"

Josie kept shaking her head. "I can't take her back. I won't. If you came here to make me, well, then I'll have to leave again."

Josiah stepped forward. "Josie, do not do that. It's not safe and you are still not strong. You will come and live with me until we can figure this out."

"I won't do that either," the girl said. "I left her for Miss Naomi. I want Miss Naomi and you to take care of her. She's better off with you both. Not me."

"Naomi loves Dinah," Raesha said, bobbing her head. "But she is concerned that you left the child with us. We wish you'd come inside with Dinah. You would have been *wilkum* in our home."

"I couldn't stay," Josie replied. "I… I don't belong with the Amish anymore."

Josiah stepped forward. "Josie, don't say that. You can find your way back to your faith."

"You don't understand. It's too late for that." She lifted her eyes to Raesha. "Promise me you will let Dinah stay with you."

Raesha sent Josiah a worried glance. "We will take care of her for as long as needed but… she is your child."

Even as she said the words, Raesha knew

it was the truth. She wouldn't hope to keep a mother from her child. But she had to understand. "Why did you decide Naomi should raise Dinah?"

Josie heaved a sob, her eyes on Raesha. "She was kind to our *mamm*...before. She would help us when she could and she always hugged me and told me I could come to her for anything. Always. I knew she'd take care of the baby. I want Dinah to stay with her. I didn't know you were there. But I'm glad now."

Josiah shot Raesha a confused gaze and touched his sister's arm. "Are you saying you don't want your own child, Josie?"

Josie's sobs escalated. She buried her face in her hands and heaved. Then she looked at Raesha, terror in her eyes. "Don't make me take her back. You can love her and care for her. Please don't make me take her back. I know I'm horrible and I can never return to my home but don't make me do this."

Raesha pulled the girl into her arms and held her there, her hand moving down Josie's hair. "Shh. It will be all right. I will take care of Dinah, I promise." Then she lifted up to face the girl. "And you are *wilkum* to come and stay with your *brudder* in the *grossdaddi haus*. When you are able. We will not disturb you there."

Josie held tight to Raesha, soaking her dress with tears. "I don't want to see the *bobbeli*. I can't see her. Ever."

Josiah looked defeated, his hat in his hand, tears in his eyes. "What can we do?"

Raesha didn't let go of the heartbroken girl. She held tight and looked up at Josiah. The agony she saw in his face only reflected the agony she felt in her heart.

Her gaze holding his, she said, "We will do what we can, when *she* is ready. But, Josie, we are not going to let you go back out there alone, do you hear me?"

The girl nodded, her head on Raesha's shoulder, her sobs slowly turning to silent weeping.

Raesha lifted Josie's chin. "Let's get you back into bed so you can rest. I will sit with you for a while and we'll see if you feel up to having a light meal."

Josie didn't argue. She crawled into the bed and let Raesha put a blanket over her.

"Rest," Josiah said, his hand stroking her arm. "I'm so sorry, Josephine."

Raesha touched Josie's forehead. "No matter what, Josie, your brother loves you and wants you well. And I do, too."

The girl closed her eyes and went silent.

Raesha walked with Josiah out into the hallway. "I will stay with her. Why don't you go and find something to eat."

"What is going on?" he asked, his eyes bright with unshed tears.

"I don't know," Raesha admitted. "But whatever it is, your sister is in no shape to take care of a child right now."

After Josiah walked away, his shoulders down, Raesha went back inside and sat down in the chair by the bed, her eyes on the frail young woman who slept there.

But she had to wonder.

What had happened to Josie to make her so afraid of her own child?

Chapter Sixteen

Josiah saw the doctor out in the hallway.

"Dr. Caldwell, do you have a minute?"

The young doctor turned and greeted Josiah. "Mr. Fisher, good to see you again. Did the nurses tell you Josie can go home tomorrow?"

Josiah shook his head. "*Neh.* We went straight to her room. A friend came with me today. Raesha Bawell, the woman who found Josie's baby."

"Ah, I see. A woman's touch."

"I think I made things worse by bringing her. Josie wants nothing to do with her baby."

"I wanted to talk to you about that, since Josie gave us permission to share her medical files with you."

"Is there something else wrong with my sister?"

"Yes, I'm afraid so. She's healing physically but she'll need to eat good hearty foods and try to exercise and get fresh air. That's not what I'm concerned about."

"What should I know about?"

"Your sister needs some counseling to help her emotionally."

"I can see that. She's upset about something."

Dr. Caldwell pulled him aside. "I don't know for sure since she won't talk about it, but I believe your sister suffered an assault. I think someone forced her."

Josiah appreciated the doctor's discretion. "I thought so, too, but I was afraid to even ask."

"Don't mention it to her," the doctor replied. "But she refuses to name the father of the baby and she told us that he's not in the baby's life."

"And she doesn't want the baby," Josiah said, dread filling his heart. "Maybe because the child reminds her of what happened to her?"

"I think so." Dr. Caldwell touched Josiah's shoulder. "I hear the Campton Center has resources for the Amish. We have their pamphlets here at the nurses' station. You can probably find a counselor there."

"I'll do that," Josiah said, weary with all the responsibility falling on his shoulder, but glad to accept it. "The center helped us with all of this so maybe they can help Josie, too."

The doctor went on to explain her medication and her follow-up visits. "Make sure she stays on course. We don't want her pneumonia to return."

Josiah thanked the doctor and then turned to go back to the room. He wasn't very hungry anyway.

When he opened the door, Josie was awake and Raesha sat smiling at her. Both women looked up when he came in.

"*Gut* news," he said. "You are being released tomorrow."

Raesha's smile brightened. "That's wonderful."

But Josie looked frightened and tearful. "Where will I go?"

Josiah wanted her with him but before he could mention that, Raesha spoke up. "You can stay with your brother in the small house he's renting from us if you want. It has a back porch that faces away from the main house. It's private there and you'll have a view of the covered bridge off in the distance."

Josie didn't look so sure.

"Or there is the Campton Center."

"What's that?" Josie asked.

Raesha rushed on. "It's a huge estate house that is now a place where we can go and get advice without having to pay much or nothing at all. They have rooms there for just such circumstances."

"I'm a circumstance?" Josie said, reminding Josiah of her old spunk.

"You are a sick young woman who is afraid to return to her people," Raesha said, reminding him of *her* spunk. "If you stay there, you'll have a staff around the clock to…help you."

"And it's close to us," Josiah added, hoping Josie might consider that and then maybe later, she could move in with him. "I can visit you every day."

Josie slipped down, the covers almost touching her chin. "I don't want to see the baby."

"You won't have to do that until you're ready," Raesha said, her hand tight over Josie's. "You'll be in a safe, beautiful place and you can come and visit Josiah or he'll come there to see you. I'll visit you as often as I can."

Josie lay there staring up at the ceiling tiles. "I just want some peace. I'm not ready to face anyone."

Nor was she ready to face what had happened, Josiah decided. The Campton Center could be the one place where she'd be able to open up and get this terrible burden out of her system so she could heal.

Because right now, she wasn't herself and the community would consider her an outsider who'd left on her own. Left and had a child without a husband to stand by her. She might be shunned and never welcomed back.

"I think the center is the best solution for now," he said. "You'll be nearby and with people who can help you, people you can talk to."

"I don't have anything to talk about," Josie replied, fear back in her eyes.

"Then don't talk," Raesha said, shooting Josiah a warning. "Just rest and read and take your time. You are always welcome in our home but if you won't feel comfortable there, I understand."

"Denke," Josie said. "I mean, thank you."

Her words tore at Josiah. She didn't think she could return to her Amish roots. But she could. He knew she could if she tried hard and asked for forgiveness. But maybe his sister didn't want to try. She seemed to have given up.

"I'll go and check with the desk," he said, "about getting you home tomorrow."

"We can stop by the Campton Center, too," Raesha said. "We'll reserve you the best room in the house, Josie."

Josie smiled at that. "A real room. That will be a blessing."

Josiah smiled for the first time since they'd arrived. Raesha had a way about her that made anyone feel better about things. He wondered how much she'd had to sacrifice by taking his sister under her wing. How much it must have hurt to know the woman she was now nurturing could one day take the baby she loved right out of her arms.

"It's all arranged," Raesha told Naomi that night. "Josie has room at the center for the next two weeks. We've set up time for counseling, too. Mrs. Campton wants to meet with Josie."

Naomi nodded. "Ah, you know she was a licensed counselor for many years before they both retired. She still helps out now and then. She was a tremendous help to Jeremiah Weaver when he came home."

"And look at him now, married with a new baby boy, happy and a strong member of our community," Raesha said.

"The Lord's work. Jeremiah did his part. He dedicated his life to his faith and his *Gott*."

Raesha moved about the kitchen, her mind on Josie coming home tomorrow. "Josiah is beside himself about what to do. I think she needs time to heal in her soul, too."

"This baby," Naomi said. "I take it she did not love the father."

"I don't think she knew the father, to be truthful," Raesha said. "I think someone took terrible advantage of her and now she has to be the one to pay for that person's sin."

"This man forced himself on her?"

"I think so. She is not ready to tell us what happened."

"I hope it wasn't the man who wanted to marry her."

Raesha stopped stirring the soup she'd made. "I don't think so. Josiah said she was happy and in love with Tobias and that he loved her, too."

Naomi's eyes went wide. "That is why she left Kentucky, then. She is ashamed of what happened to her and she felt she could not marry the man she loved."

"That is heartbreaking," Raesha said. "I resented her, you know. For deserting her child, for not taking responsibility. But after meeting her today and seeing her agony, I only felt sympathy for her and now I truly want to help her."

Naomi buttered rolls they'd baked yesterday. "That is why *Gott* allowed her to leave Dinah with us. The baby is being cared for, but the mother is in need of our prayers and forgiveness. We can help bring this girl back to her faith so she can have a *gut* life, here or somewhere far from here."

"You always see things in a different light," Raesha said, understanding that this task would not be easy.

"I see what the Lord puts before me," Naomi replied. "So many things."

Raesha felt the imprint of that last remark. Her mother-in-law thought she and Josiah made a good match. They were friends and now they were being pushed together even more.

But her heart wasn't ready to explore her feelings for Josiah. So much between them, so many things to overcome.

The Lord will see me through as He always has, she thought.

"The soup is ready," she announced. "I'll go and find Josiah."

"And I'll check in on Dinah," Naomi said, going over to the baby's crib. "Awake and alert. What a sweetheart."

Raesha thought about the baby they'd come to love and she also thought about the man she was beginning to care a lot about. It seemed so simple. They could make a perfect family and yet, there was no perfection here. Only the Lord held perfection.

For so long now, she'd dreamed of a family, of children laughing and her husband coming home to give her a presupper kiss. Aaron had done that. He'd loved her and cherished her and tried to be the best husband possible.

Not perfect but the best.

Now she could see a new future just out of her reach.

She wouldn't look past today. She wouldn't try to second-guess the Lord's plan for her.

But she sure would like to know what else could change in her life.

When she knocked on Josiah's door, she was surprised to find Nathan Craig standing there with him. "Mr. Craig, it is *gut* to see you again."

"Hello, Mrs. Bawell," the Englischer said. "It's good to see you, too. Josiah is getting me up-to-date on Josie."

"Yes, we're thrilled she is leaving the hospital."

Josiah looked sheepish but nodded. "I wanted Mr. Craig to find out about the father of her child."

Raesha understood. "I see. Do you think that is wise?"

"I only want to know his name," Josiah replied. "I will not tell him about Dinah."

"I think that's best for now," she replied. "He might force the baby away."

"Or he might not want any responsibilities," Mr. Craig said, his eyes going dark.

"I want to know who he is," Josiah said. "Amish or Englisch."

"What will that help?" Raesha asked.

"It will help me," Josiah replied, his tone firm.

She wouldn't question him further. This was

his business, not hers. But she was caught in the middle of it so she was glad he'd confided in her.

"Supper is ready," she announced. "Mr. Craig, please come and have some beef-and-vegetable soup with us."

Nathan Craig looked surprised. "You know, that sounds good on this bright, chilly night. Thank you."

"You are always *wilkum*," she replied.

She wished she could hear this man's story. He wore his troubles as a map on his face. But a map that had many roads.

So much was changing in her world, but Raesha decided she'd stay steadfast and lean on the Lord.

And she'd stay busy. She had much to do over the next few days. Too busy to worry about what she could not control.

Josiah smiled at her as they made their way to the house. "Josie will be nearby this time tomorrow. I hope she won't leave us again."

"I hope that, too," she replied.

She did not want the girl to come to any more harm and she couldn't bear seeing the man she cared about being in such agony again.

"This is a *gut* day," Josiah said the next afternoon, looking so young and relaxed Raesha couldn't help but feel the same way. Josiah needed something uplifting to boost his spirits, and getting Josie settled at the Campton Center had done just that.

"We give thanks to the Father," she replied, knowing that God had provided for little Dinah and now for Josie, too.

Now they had to do the same.

"Do you think Josie will be okay here?" he asked, taking in the big room and attached bathroom. "This is much more than we are used to." He motioned to the bathroom where Josie had gone.

Raesha wondered how Josie would react to meeting Judy Campton. The elderly woman made quite a statement in her quiet, dignified way. Because her assistant and lifelong friend, Bettye Willis, had Amish roots, Mrs. Campton had made it her business to always support the Amish of Campton Creek. And they all returned the favor by watching out for her and this stately old mansion.

Taking in the big bed with the ornate headboard and the comfortable floral chairs near a bay window that overlooked the pool and sweeping backyard, Raesha realized Josie's life would never be the same. But then, neither would Josiah's. She would help him take care of his little family, but what would she do if he took Josie and baby Dinah back to Ohio?

When Josie came out of the bathroom, walking slowly and looking pale, she stood and took in the room. "I... I don't know what to think. I have lived in many places since I left Kentucky but this one reminds me of a castle."

"Do you like it?" Josiah asked, worry in his words.

"What's not to like?" his sister said. Dressed in jeans and a too-big blue sweater that Raesha had found on sale at the general store, she moved around the room. "I need the privacy and I love looking out at the garden."

"You have a couple of weeks here," Josiah said. "So you can heal and talk to people who understand."

"Do you think I've lost my mind?" Josie asked, her tone bordering on harsh.

"Neh," he replied. "I think you've lost your way."

Josie walked to the window and stared out.

A knock at the door brought her head around.

Raesha moved to answer and found Bettye pushing Mrs. Campton in a wheelchair.

"Hello," Bettye said. "Mrs. C wanted to meet all of you right away." She nodded to the white-haired woman in the chair.

"It's so nice to have you here, Josie," Mrs. Campton said, her gnarled fingers touching her pearls. "And Mr. Fisher and Mrs. Bawell, so good of you to help Josie through this."

Josie stared at Judy Campton, fear in her eyes. "I'm not sure what I'm doing here, but this is a lovely place."

"It's a healing place," Judy said after Bettye left. "You have been through a lot and now your only task is to rest and talk to me."

"So you think there is something wrong with me?" the young girl asked, defiance in her eyes.

"I think there is something wrong with a world where a young girl thinks she can't come home again," Mrs. Campton replied without missing a beat.

Josie didn't smart off at that remark. "I guess I can tolerate it for a few days."

"I think you will find our place very reassuring and safe," Mrs. Campton said. "Let's all sit down and I'll explain how this works."

Raesha sank onto a brocade footstool, feeling small and out of place. But she listened as Judy Campton told Josie about the rules—curfews and no wandering away. She was free to come and go, but she had to let someone know at all times and she had to be back by eight each night.

"Do you think I'll run away again?" Josie asked.

"Do you want to run away again?" Mrs. Campton countered.

Josie glanced at her brother and then to Raesha. "I don't think so. But I won't stay where I don't belong."

"Then together, you and I will figure out where you do belong," Judy Campton replied.

Raesha could see why this woman helped people get their lives back together. She smiled without judgment and listened without condemning. A lesson for anyone.

Josie sat back in her chair. "I'm tired."

"Then you must rest," Mrs. Campton said. "Supper is at six thirty sharp." She looked Josie over. "Do you prefer Englisch clothing or Amish?"

"Englisch," Josie blurted out. Then she hastily added, "For now."

"For now, it is," Judy replied. "I'll have one of our volunteers show you the clothing room."

Soon after that, Josie curled up in the comfortable bed and closed her eyes. Josiah wheeled Mrs. Campton to the elevator she'd had installed.

"Bettye will meet me upstairs," she said after thanking him. "This takes me to the hallway and then to the garage apartment. Very convenient."

"We appreciate what you are doing," Josiah said.

"We have a lot to work through with that

one," Judy replied, her words kind. "But we will get there."

On the ride home, Josiah turned to Raesha. "Do you think she'll stay there? Maybe I should have insisted on bringing her home with us."

Raesha didn't have the answer for that. "You have to decide where home is, I think. And then you must convince Josie that she needs to be with family, wherever that might be."

He sent Raesha a perplexed glance. "*Ja*, I wish I could figure that out."

"Give it time," she replied. Because she wished he could figure that out, too.

But she wished he'd pick here for his home.

Chapter Seventeen

Festival day dawned chilly and windy, but soon the sun was out and the crowds started pouring through. Vehicles parked in designated fields along the main road and filled up parking spaces in town. Neighbors lined up with their wares, some in booths and some with long tables near the road.

Josiah met up with her at the double tent the Bawell Hat Shop had set up in the yard near the dirt driveway. "This is a big event," he said, taking in the buggies and cars lined up along the yard and road. "You have a large selection of things to sell."

"We work toward this all year," she explained with pride. "Spring and fall." Lifting a basket of jellies and jams, she started toward the booth.

"Here, let me," he said, taking it from her to walk with her. "Do you enjoy this?"

"I do," she admitted. "I love talking to neighbors and selling them things they need—quilts, canned goods, crocheted items, and hats and bonnets, of course. Some save up just to buy a good hat."

He tugged at his own. "I think I need to get a new one."

Raesha smiled at that. He didn't know she'd already been working on a new winter hat for him. She'd sneaked the measurements from one of his old hats she'd found on the *grossdaddi haus* porch.

"We'll see what can be done," she quipped after he'd handed off the basket to Susan. "After this, we get ready for the Christmas season. The Englisch love to buy Amish gifts for friends and family. So it never ends."

"How do you do it?" he asked, admiration in his gaze.

Raesha stopped in a spot away from the action beneath the shade of an old oak by the shop's porch. "I told you, I love this. I know I'm different from most and some of the men here frown on me being a businesswoman, but... Aaron never minded. He relished the way I took charge and helped him out in the shop. He always wanted to be outside doing farmwork so when I slowly started taking over, he got to do more of what he truly loved."

"And you discovered you enjoyed being the boss?"

She saw the amused smile that came with that question.

"I had to learn to be the boss, *ja*. But I also realized I have a good head for business and what I didn't know, I learned. I can make a hat from start to finish because I want to know what my employees go through each day. I've learned every aspect of hat-making and running a gift shop."

"You are amazing," he said, his eyes full of a warmth that took away the chill of the wind. "Mr. Hartford said you plied him with questions about such things. He's very proud of you."

"He understands how business works," she replied, happy to hear that news. "He works hand in hand with all of us and provides us with specialty items that we use and need."

"I'm impressed," Josiah said, glancing around. "You managed to find help with Dinah today and yet, you keep checking on her and me. Thanks to you and Naomi, my niece is growing strong."

"She is so precious," Raesha said. "I get a burst of joy each time she smiles at me."

"I do, too."

It had been two days since they'd left Josie

at the center. "Have you heard from your sister today, Josiah?"

"Not yet," he admitted. "I invited her to the festival when I was there yesterday but she said no. She seems to prefer sitting by the window and watching the birds in the garden."

"Time spent in quiet is always healing," Raesha replied. "I hope to visit her Sunday afternoon, if that's okay."

"You can go with me," he suggested. "If that's okay with you, that is."

Raesha laughed. "We need to stop being so polite about things. You know I'll do whatever I can to help."

His eyes held hers, and all the commotion around them seemed to slip away. "And you know that I want you with me."

Raesha's heart fluttered against her apron.

Looking away, he added, "I mean, when I visit Josie."

Disappointment stopped her heart and settled her. "Of course. I'll plan on it."

She turned to get back to work, but Josiah stopped her. "Raesha…"

"I understand," she said, not wanting to hear any explanations or excuses. "I have work to do."

Hurrying away, Raesha stiffened her spine and concluded that Josiah Fisher was off-limits to her. At least until he could decide whether he wanted her in his life or not. But then, she had to decide the same about him, too.

Josiah helped where he could and tried to stay out of the way. The Bawell Hat Shop was a popular destination. The booth had stayed busy all day and the door to the shop jingled in a constant melody. No time to track down Raesha and try to salvage the connection they'd almost made earlier.

Now as the festival drew to an end, the afternoon sunshine waned and the air grew cold. Time to finish up.

He did his part by carrying tables and chairs back to the storage area in the big barn, putting away tent canvases and taking up stakes. This work didn't require much thinking, so he stayed silent and hurried along.

But Raesha had extra help and she had everything under control. While he admired those traits in her, he also wished she'd open up to him and let him get a little closer to her.

He wanted to know her heart. Did she have feelings for him? Or was he imagining what could never be?

Now he stood on the tiny porch of the little house that had become his home, his mind on going to see Josie tomorrow. His sister's smile had returned but she still had that dark, faraway look in her pretty hazel eyes.

"I can't discuss what she and I talk about," Judy Campton told him yesterday. "But I will say that she is blessed to have survived all she's been through. She hasn't told me everything but I can tell from her silence that she is suffering greatly."

Josiah left it at that, his many questions still unanswered. He wanted the truth but he had not heard from Nathan Craig so now he waited, his patience running thin and his heart growing weary with doubt and apprehension.

Deciding he'd go and get Dinah early, he came around the house and saw a group of men finishing up with removing some of the other tables and booths along the road.

Samuel Troyer waved him over. "Josiah, what have you decided about setting up your barn raising?"

Surprised, Josiah shook his head. "I hoped to get the house finished up but a new barn is in my plans."

"Winter is coming," Samuel replied, his tone calm. "Need to get it up in the next few weeks or you'll have to wait until spring."

Josiah thought about that and then he considered his limited budget. "I can't afford a big barn. I'd thought to build a smaller one with a loft and room for a horse and buggy."

"We can get that done," Samuel replied. "Talk to Mr. Hartford. He has discount lumber lying around everywhere but it's good wood. We can add in the rest."

"I'll do that," Josiah said. "Then there is the matter of my sister. She is improving but I'm not sure what to do when she is ready to leave the Campton Center."

"Can the girl stay with you?" Samuel asked.

Josiah thought this man would give him the answers he sought. "I hope so. But…will she be shunned?"

"We will discuss this with the bishop," Samuel suggested. "Bishop King has noticed that you and Raesha seem to be close."

Who hadn't noticed that?

"We are friends. She is a big help to me with the little one."

"You have a lot going on," Samuel noted. "I pray you can do what needs to be done."

"I am trying my best."

"I'm here if you need advice."

Josiah nodded. "*Denke.* I want my family whole again. I'm praying toward that end."

Samuel looked toward the house. "Well, you have two very strong champions on your side."

"You mean the Bawell women."

Samuel smiled. "You could do worse."

"I could," Josiah admitted. "But I'm not sure what to do about that. The one I'm interested in might not feel the same about me. Besides, I've always shied away from marriage."

"And why is that?" Samuel asked.

Josiah had never voiced it before. "I don't want to wind up like my *daed*," he said, the admission lifting a great weight off his shoulders.

If Samuel was surprised, he didn't show it. "What makes you think that could happen?"

"I don't know. I've heard bad traits can be inherited."

"Not if you ask God to give you a pure heart and grace to get on with your life," Samuel replied. "I've seen that heart in you, son. And that grace. Don't let something good slip away because you can't forgive the man who brought you into the world."

Josiah didn't know what to say but his brain brightened as if a gas lamp had been lit inside his head. "I'll let you know about the barn raising, Mr. Troyer."

"Ready when you are," Samuel replied. "As for your sister, I hope she will turn back to her Amish family and find her faith again. Part of letting go of the past is looking to the future with hope."

Josiah wanted to have that kind of hope. But he was afraid it would be an uphill battle.

Visiting Sunday always brought Raesha a sense of excitement. Sometimes, friends would come by and sit with Naomi and her for the afternoon. They'd talk about life, read a bit of the Scriptures and sing favorite hymns.

Today, she would be doing the visiting. As planned, she was going to the Campton Center with Josiah to see his sister. Dinah was all tucked in while some of Naomi's friends came to sit with her and watch over the baby. By now, the whole community knew about little Dinah and anyone who saw her fell in love with her.

But they still weren't sure about Josiah and how much time he was spending with Raesha.

"Are people talking?" he asked now as he helped her up onto the buggy, Chester lifting his hoofs in impatience.

"People always talk," she replied. "If you're worried about the three women who are probably staring out the kitchen window at us, let them stare. We've done nothing wrong."

"We are friends," he added, sounding as if he were trying to convince himself of that status.

"*Ja*, friends who are trying to take care of a child and a troubled young woman."

"Do you ever wish I'd not come into your life?"

Glancing over at him as Chester took them up the long drive to the road, Raesha shook her head. "Why would I wish such a thing?"

"Because Dinah and I have interfered in your life."

"Dinah is not an interference," she retorted, clearly appalled. "But you on the other hand…"

Josiah shot her a frown only to find her smiling.

"You are a cruel woman, Raesha Bawell. You tease because you like me, right?"

"I like you well enough," she admitted, trying to keep things light.

"You know, a lot of people have hinted to me that you and I…would make a good match."

Shocked, Raesha ignored the heated blush moving down her face. "People should mind their own business."

Josiah looked frustrated and tried again. "But they make a *gut* case. We are both single and… I need a woman's touch."

Raesha almost gulped in fear but that comment brought her back to reality. Was he about to propose? "Are you serious?"

"I'm contemplating," he said, the look of utter confusion in his gaze making her almost laugh. "I'm trying to be logical but I know you don't want to leave Naomi."

"And you're not sure you will stay in Campton Creek."

He clicked the reins and got a snort from Chester. "Then there is Josie to consider."

"You want her with you, but she doesn't want to be around her own child."

The playful mood shifted at about the same time the wind blew cold across Raesha's burning skin.

"It's something to consider," he said on a deflated note.

"Why don't we take this one step at a time," she finally replied. "Josie needs to get well, in both mind and body, and you still have to fix up the farmhouse and barn to sell."

"You're right. Logical at that."

"The one constant is Dinah. She is not a burden, Josiah. I love her."

Josiah gave her a look that said nothing but told her everything. She'd made it sound as if she cared for only the *bobbeli*.

Raesha wanted to shout to him that she cared for him, too. Too much. But she wouldn't give him false hope. She could not up and move to Ohio or anywhere else. Josiah had a lot of decisions to make, and most of them involved keeping his sister and her child with him.

Which meant Raesha might be left out,

even if she wanted to be with him and his little family forever.

They sat with Josie in the big sunroom where they could see the old camellias in the Campton Center garden.

"I made cookies," Josie said when they arrived. "And I can make hot tea for us."

They both asked for tea since she seemed so eager.

"She looks better," Josiah said when she hurried away to the kitchen on the other side of the house.

"I think being here has helped her," Raesha replied, glad to see him relax a bit.

Glancing around, she took in the white wicker furniture and the lush ferns on each side of the big room that was mostly windows and doors. Other exotic plants sat here and there, reminding her of the opulence of this huge house.

"I can see why Josie might love it here," she whispered to Josiah. "It's very relaxing and... beautiful."

"This community is blessed to have such a place," he replied. "The Englisch here seem to accept us."

"That has never been a problem," she assured him. "We work with them, side by side."

He looked over at Raesha, his dark eyes

full of hope. "We could make it work, I think. Bringing her back to your place, with me. I hope since she was never baptized, the bishop will allow that."

Raesha wanted that, too. "What if she gets upset about Dinah?"

He mulled that over. "We'll keep them apart."

Raesha wondered if that was any way to live but she'd cross that bridge when she came to it. Josie didn't seem in a hurry to leave the luxury of Campton House. Raesha had a feeling the girl might want to stay out here in the world, but that could be because she was ashamed to return to her roots.

"Only if you feel comfortable with that," he said in a hurry. "The old house is ready but I don't know how she feels about the place."

Raesha wanted to respond but Josie came back in, carrying a silver tray with a teapot and cups on it.

After she served tea and cookies, she sat down. Today, she wore a pretty button-up sweater and a flowing floral skirt over some sort of boots, her hair pulled back in a stern ponytail.

"I might get a job here," she announced. "Mrs. Campton needs someone to help with the baking and kitchen work."

"Do you want to work here?" Josiah asked, concern marring his earlier happiness.

"Yes," Josie said, her tone firm. "I don't think I want to return to the Amish, brother."

Josiah looked at Raesha, the hurt inside his heart shining brightly in his dark eyes. She gave him an encouraging stare.

"There is plenty of time to consider that," she said, hoping to diffuse the situation.

"I don't need time," Josie retorted. "No one will want me back and… I'm okay with that. I can work here and stay in an apartment here in town."

"It seems you've thought this out," Josiah said. "I only ask that you consider this very carefully before you make a rash decision."

"It's my decision to make," Josie said. "Have another cookie."

Josiah took a sugar cookie but held it in his hand. "I'm glad you're feeling better," he told his sister. "But I think we need to head back. The weather is getting worse."

With that, they left after visiting his sister for only a few minutes.

"You're right," he told Raesha once they were in the buggy again. "I have a lot to work out before I can even consider getting on with my life."

Raesha didn't know what to say. But a future with him seemed impossible at this point.

Chapter Eighteen

October turned the fields fallow and the trees golden and burgundy. A soft rain covered the countryside this morning.

Josiah stood on the little porch of the place he had come to think of as home and stared across at the house where he'd grown up. He had two days to decide where Josie would live. There with him or here with him and the Bawell women.

And Dinah.

She still wanted to live in town and work at the Campton Center. He'd talked to the bishop Samuel Weaver by his side to guide him and vouch for him.

"Your sister can return but she will have to accept the tenets of her faith—our ways—Josiah. If she fails again, she will not be able to come back."

Samuel nodded. "You must make her understand that she will not be shunned as long as she confesses all and gives her life back to *Gott*."

"But she was attacked," he explained. "This is not her fault."

"We understand that," Bishop King said. "Still, she left the child here and ran away and she's been through things we don't know about. It's best for her to start fresh."

"I will explain all of this to her," Josiah promised. "I cannot predict if she will accept or not."

He knew if Josie decided to stay with the Englisch, he'd have limited contact with her. But he would not give up on his sister.

He hoped to convince her to come home with him.

But he wasn't sure where his real home might be.

The rain increased but he stood still, his heart hurting for the life he'd had inside that house. He should have stayed and protected Josie. That regret would stay with him until his dying day.

Then the door behind him opened.

Raesha stood there, wet and shaking. "I looked all over for you. Everywhere."

"What's wrong?"

"The shop— I got a call that you need to go to the Campton Center. Mrs. Campton said Josie has had a breakthrough and she's asking for you."

Josiah remembered other phone calls. "This could be good news, then."

Raesha bobbed her head. "It could be. Or…it could mean she's not coming back to us. Ever."

"I'll go and see what has happened."

She nodded, so used to this. So used to having to tell him bad and good news and then take care of Dinah for him.

He loved Raesha. He could see that now, here in the cold rain. She had run through that rain, searching for him because she always did the right thing. Even if her heart was breaking.

He wanted to say so much to her.

But he had to go.

"I'll be back soon, I hope."

"Take your time. We'll be right here."

Waiting.

She would wait.

But one day, she'd get tired of waiting.

"She has told me everything," Judy Campton said when Josiah came into Alisha Braxton's office. "Now it's time for her to tell you. She realizes that and is willing to be honest with you." Mrs. Campton sat in a chair across from Alisha, weariness showing in her sagging shoulders.

The lady lawyer's eyes held sympathy. "After you talk to Josie, if you need me for anything, Mr. Fisher…"

"Denke," Josiah said, already heading out the office for the stairs to Josie's room. Then he turned back to Judy Campton. "And *denke* for working to heal my sister. Go and rest now."

"I think I shall do that," Judy Campton said, her expression serene now. "I'm getting too old for this, I think."

Josiah decided he'd aged ten years himself.

But he took a deep breath and prayed for strength. Because he didn't know what his sister would say to him. Then he knocked on the door.

"Come in."

Her voice sounded strong but when he saw her, he could tell she'd been through the wringer. Josie looked wiped out and so tired.

"Josie?"

"Let me talk, brother," she said. "Let me get it all out, please."

"All right."

He sat down across from her and remained silent.

"In Kentucky, we hung around with some *Englisch* kids who were the same age as us.

Tobias—the man I was to marry—knew one of them. They were good friends."

She stopped, stared out the window, her hands clutching the bright fabric of the chair. "Drew seemed so nice and I tolerated him because Tobias admired him. They worked the land together."

Josiah wanted to hit something or someone. He hated the terror that edged her calm words. "What happened?"

She lifted her head. "Drew drugged my drink one night and…took advantage of me. I woke up in a room in his house and… I knew something bad had happened. But I went home to the place where I stayed with some other girls. I told them I'd spent the night with an Englisch girl at her home. But they knew. They had to know."

Josiah had so many questions but he stayed still and silent.

"I never told Tobias the truth but I stopped going to Drew's house after that. I told Tobias it didn't feel right. He never questioned me but I did notice he didn't go there as much after that either."

Holding a hand to her face, she went on. "We were planning our wedding. Two months until I'd become Tobias's wife."

The sobs came softly but she kept talking.

"I started feeling sick all the time, throwing up. One of my friends asked me if I could be pregnant.

"I tried to deny it. Told them I had a stomach virus. But I went to the midwife and she confirmed it. I was pregnant and… I knew Drew had to be the father."

Josiah sat up, his hands falling against his knees. "I'm so sorry, Josephine. So sorry I wasn't there to watch out for you."

She wiped at her eyes. "Tobias loved me. He watched out for me but…he didn't know that his best friend had done this horrible thing. I panicked. I was so embarrassed and afraid and ashamed. I ran away and found work and a room and when I had enough money, I tried to get to Ohio but then I realized I'd be shunned there."

Standing, she paced before the window, her arms held against her stomach, a solid shield. "I managed to catch a bus to Pennsylvania and… I think you know the rest."

"You stayed in a small settlement not far from here," Josiah replied. "Had your baby at the hospital and then tried to take care of Dinah on your own."

"But I was too sick, Josiah. I was too sick and…traumatized. I remembered Mrs.

Bawell. How kind she was when we were living next door."

Josiah stood and stopped his sister's pacing. "You did what you had to do, Josie. But what about Tobias? You could have explained to him."

"No, I could not." Pulling away, she shook her head. "I could not tell him what his friend did, Josiah. I was too ashamed. I was afraid no one would believe me."

"That boy needs to be punished."

"He has been," she said. "I got word from a friend who didn't know about what he'd done to me. She was just gossiping but she wrote to me and told me he'd been arrested for doing the same thing to another girl—this one Englisch and with a powerful father. He went to jail. He will be there for a long time. I don't want you to do anything, hear me?"

"I hear you," Josiah said, thankful for justice. "Still I'd like to pummel his head."

"You don't mean that."

He did but he'd pray on that matter.

"Do you believe me?" she asked, her voice wobbling. "I need you to believe me."

"I believe you," he replied. "And I'm sorry, so sorry. But you can come home now. You can come back to your faith."

"I don't know if I can do that," she said,

anger coloring her words. "Do you see what I have become?"

"I see my sister and I love you."

"I'm flawed, damaged. I'll never be well."

"I will help you. We will all help you."

"You and Raesha Bawell. The woman who wants to keep my baby?"

"She wants what's best for Dinah. We all do."

"Well, I'm not what's best for Dinah. I can't bear to look at her."

"She is an innocent child, Josie."

"I was once an innocent child, too. But not anymore."

"Josie, you can be forgiven and accepted again. It's different here. People are less strict. Not like—"

"Not like our father?" She looked surprised.

"I'm telling you, the Bawells won't judge you."

"But the rest of them will."

"I don't think so. I will protect you."

His sister gave him a look that chilled him. She didn't believe him because he had already failed her.

Raesha waited by the window, watching for Josiah. Would he bring Josie back here or would she stay at the center and find a job in town?

"My life used to be so simple."

"You know you are way too young to be talking to yourself," Naomi said from behind her. "Talk to me instead."

"This man," Raesha said, lifting her hands up. "He's so hard to understand. I can't decide if he likes me or hates me or wants me in his life or just needs me to take care of his niece."

Naomi stood by the kitchen table, steady as a rock. "I think he likes you, a lot. I think he wants you in his life. And I think he needs you to help with his niece but he feels badly about asking."

"You're taking his side?"

"I didn't know there was a side."

Raesha pulled out the frying pan to make a light supper. "Scrambled eggs and biscuits."

"Perfect," Naomi replied. "But you hate scrambled eggs."

"I'll eat biscuits. With ham."

Naomi went to her chair and smiled and talked baby talk to Dinah. "Hard to believe she's been with us for one month now."

"She's growing up fast."

"She's already trying to roll over. In a month or two, she'll be so proud of herself."

Raesha stopped beating eggs and walked over to look down at the gurgling, smiling infant. Dinah had been gifted with so many girlie baby gowns, the child would never get around to wearing all of them. Today, they'd dressed her in a blue broadcloth dress with smocking across the front and a white crocheted bonnet that couldn't contain her brown curls. Her little feet were covered in dark blue bootie socks.

Touching on one of her kicking feet, Raesha said, "She is so beautiful. Why does she have to be so beautiful?"

"*Gott* made her that way."

Pulling her hand away, Raesha backed up. "I can't keep doing this. I'm going to tell Josiah he needs to hire someone else to be his nanny."

Naomi's rocking chair creaked. "He'll have to take the money he's saving to buy lumber for the barn."

"He'll manage. He works hard and he's always picking up odd jobs to make ends meet." Raesha went to the pantry closet and uncovered the leftover biscuits from breakfast. "He helps Mr. Hartford around the store and then comes back to work on the house and tear down what remains of that barn. It's a wonder he ever gets to spend time with Dinah or Josie."

"He is industrious in that way. He wants that old farm to shine so he can get the best price for it."

Raesha buttered the biscuits and checked on the oven. "I could wait until after the barn's done, I suppose."

"It's your decision."

As usual, her astute mother-in-law had let her talk herself out of a rant. And out of finding a nanny for Dinah at that.

"I'm going to finish supper now."

"I'll sit here and chat with Dinah."

Raesha made the eggs and browned the biscuits, adding some preserves and some ham slices. It was that kind of night.

Then she heard the buggy jostling up the lane and all of her anger and frustration went right out the window.

Josiah was back. But he wasn't alone.

His sister, Josie, was in the buggy with him.

"How did you convince her to come?"

Raesha sat with Josiah at the kitchen table. Naomi had gone to bed and now he was holding Dinah and feeding her a bedtime bottle. They'd agreed that the baby would stay with Raesha and Naomi for now since Josie refused to see her.

"It wasn't easy. She thinks she can't come back but I told her this place is different."

"We are very forgiving around here."

"She is ashamed and frightened so she uses a bad attitude to cover that up."

"I can understand that. What she must have

gone through. I wish this man could be taught a lesson."

"I wanted that, too. But he is behind bars. I'll have Nathan Craig confirm that for our peace of mind. And so I won't go and find the man and kill him with my bare hands."

"Josiah, you know that is not our way."

"It's *my* way," he retorted with such anger, Dinah's eyelashes fluttered up from dozing.

"You can't go after this man. That won't change what has happened."

"I want to teach him a lesson but that might upset Josie even more." Carefully passing Dinah back to Raesha, he said, "I'd better go and check on her. She was worn-out when we got home."

"Take her some food," Raesha said, indicating the plate she'd made up for both of them. "She needs nourishment."

"She needs a lot of things but Mrs. Campton thinks the worst is over. She told me to just love her and let her be."

"*Gut* advice."

Taking the plate, he stared over at Raesha, his brown eyes burning coals. "I'm going to give you extra rent money to cover Josie's up-keep and to show you how much I appreciate your help with all of this."

"Don't insult me," she replied on a loud whisper. "I don't mind you paying honest rent but I refuse to charge you for taking care of Dinah or helping Josie. Stop that nonsense."

"Why are you so stubborn?"

"Why are you so dense?"

Raesha held Dinah close but he inched forward. When the baby let out a soft whimper since they'd scared her awake, Josiah shook his head and backed away.

"We will discuss this more later."

"You don't owe me any money, Josiah."

"I owe you everything," he replied. Then he turned around and stomped to the door. "And I have nothing to give you."

After he left, Raesha sat down in the rocker and held Dinah close to lull her back to sleep. "He has more to give than anyone I've ever known," she whispered to the drowsy little baby. "I just need to convince him of that."

Chapter Nineteen

Raesha braced herself. She wanted to go and see Josie but she had to tread lightly here. The girl had been with Josiah for three days now but Raesha had not seen her. She'd tried to give Josie the time and space she needed. But now, the girl needed some clothes.

Josiah had gone to meet with Bishop King, Samuel and Jeremiah going with him to offer support and assure the bishop that Josie should find her way here, not out there alone.

And while he was off doing that task, Raesha had left Dinah with Susan's younger sister Greta and Naomi cozy inside the big house. One thing about this community—everyone truly pitched in to help, especially when it involved children.

Now she had an hour to talk to Josie.

Knocking on the door of the *grossdaddi*

haus, Raesha held a basket of clothes and shoes for the girl. And a plate of blueberry muffins she'd made earlier.

"Who is it?" Josie called from behind the door.

"It's Raesha. I came to welcome you to our home."

Josie opened the door and stared at the basket. "I have clothes."

"You need these clothes," Raesha said, trying to keep her tone neutral. "May I come in? It's a chilly morning."

Josie opened the door and let her inside. Raesha set the basket on the small kitchen table and turned around. The place was clean and smelled of lemon furniture polish. Josie had rearranged a few things to make it cozy.

A good sign.

A hand on the basket, Raesha said, "There is a wool cloak and new bonnet in here and some sturdy winter shoes that should fit you. Everything you need in twos, so you can wash and change often."

"That's nice of you," Josie said, touching a finger to the wool cloak. "And I love blueberry muffins."

"Then sit and have one."

Josie grabbed a muffin and moved to the sofa by the woodstove. "This is a cozy house."

"It's a strong house," Raesha said, sitting down across from her in a high-backed oak chair with ruffled cushions. "Many people have stayed here."

"My brother says you take in people."

"When we need to, *ja*."

"I didn't want to come here."

"I know, but I'm glad you did. Your brother needs you."

"Josiah? He's never needed anyone."

"You don't really know your brother, do you?"

"Do you know him?"

"I think I'm beginning to," Raesha said. "He works hard and tries to take care of things. He wants to make everyone's life better. Meantime, he barely has time to live his own life."

"He's had plenty of time," Josie said, putting her muffin down on the table. "He went away and left me…in that house."

"He was young and he wanted a better life."

"I wanted that, too, but I didn't get to leave. And when I did have to go away, I messed up."

"Josie, you didn't mess up. Someone else is to blame for what happened to you."

"I shouldn't have been at that party that night. Tobias was there but he was downstairs in another room." She stopped, broke off some muffin. "I… I remember trying to call his name."

Every time Raesha wanted to be angry with this young woman, Josie said something that broke her heart. "You could get in touch with Tobias. I'm sure he's concerned about you."

"He's probably married now," Josie said, her voice cracking. "I should have stayed away but it was tough out there on my own. I really tried to make it. I don't want to be a burden."

Raesha saw the truth in the girl's whispered words. "Josie, do you want to be Amish again? Or would you rather stay out there in the world?"

Josie shook her head. "I don't know. I feel safe here and I miss my Amish friends. I miss Tobias. But there is no place for me now."

Raesha touched her hand to Josie's. "You have a place here, whether it's in this house or the house your brother had rebuilt. Remember that. You will always be safe here."

Josie's eyes went wide. "I don't know. I need to be alone now. I don't want to think about this."

"I'll leave you alone, then," Raesha said. "Josiah should be back soon."

Josie nodded, tears in her eyes.

"If you need me, come to the front door of the hat shop. You don't have to go through the house."

The girl didn't say anything. She sat with

her hands crossed in her lap, her hair falling across her face.

Raesha hated to leave her, but what else could she do? Pushing would only make Josie bolt. And she did not want that to happen again.

She went to the door but turned when Josie called out.

Josie stood and rubbed her hands down her sweater. "Is she happy?"

"You mean Dinah?"

The girl nodded.

"She is a sweet, pleasant baby. She is growing strong. Other than a little colic now and then, she is a fine girl."

Josie's eyes watered, tears spilling over like a current on the creek. She didn't speak but she nodded.

Raesha wanted to rush back and hug her close but she didn't do that. Josie was so fragile, one sudden move could crush her.

"I will check on you later," Raesha said.

Josie nodded and turned toward the smaller of the two bedrooms.

Raesha shut the door and left, her prayers focused on this girl's healing.

"Josie doesn't know if she's ready to seek forgiveness," Josiah told Raesha later that day. "But the bishop is willing to see this through."

"I'm thankful for that," Raesha told him, her eyes warm. He loved this time of day when they usually sat with Dinah for a few minutes before he took her across the way.

Now he couldn't do that. Josie was there.

"She should be with her mother," he said, then after seeing the hurt in Raesha's eyes, wished he hadn't.

Lowering her head, she replied, "Maybe one day."

He stared down at Dinah. The baby gurgled and kicked. Raesha had managed to find several bibs and gowns for his niece and they all made her look even more adorable.

To break the silence, he said, "I think she recognizes my voice."

"And your presence," Raesha replied, her face blank now. "She knows who you are."

"She smiles more at you, though," he offered, hoping to salvage their precious time together.

"Do you think so?"

"I do." He held Dinah's chubby fingers. "She has a firm grip." Then he looked over at Raesha. "Where is Naomi?"

"She decided to meet Josie. She went over about an hour ago to sit with her."

Seeing the fatigue in her eyes, he said, "I have burdened both of you so much."

"Do not say that again," Raesha replied, getting up to check on the pot roast cooking on the stove. "We have helped many people but we've both been blessed having Dinah here."

"People will talk and think I'm shirking my responsibilities."

"People will always talk. I know your heart."

"Do you?"

She whirled at his question, her eyes vivid with surprise. "I hope so."

Tugging up from where he'd been kneeling next to the crib, he came to stand by Raesha in the kitchen. "I wish that we could have met in a different way."

"I do, too."

"I'm not good with courting or making conversation," he admitted. "I think that is why I'm still alone. But with you, I feel *gut*. I get terrible nervous around you, but... I like being around you."

Her eyes went soft, her smile quiet. "I feel the same, Josiah. I loved my husband so much but...you have added a bit of happiness to my life."

"So it's not just about Dinah?"

"*Neh*. Dinah is a precious child. But if I'd never held her in my arms, or never known her sweetness, I'd still care about you. You are the kind of man any woman would be proud to call her own."

His heart lifted, hope flowing like a river. "Could you call me your own?"

Raesha went back to stirring the pot. "The question is—can you ever call me your own? Or will you soon go away forever?"

Josiah didn't know the answer to that question. But he did know one thing. He could so easily love this woman.

How could he reconcile that realization with what lay ahead for him?

Before he could answer that question, Naomi entered the back door and smiled at them. "Josie and I had a wonderful time getting to know each other. She invited me back."

"That's nice since it's your house," he said, misery settling over him. "How does she seem to you, Mammi Naomi?"

"Confused and shattered," Naomi replied without batting an eye. "We give her love. Lots of love. It's a cruel world and she has seen that cruelty firsthand."

"Will she ever heal?" he asked, hope hinging on the question.

"With time, maybe," Naomi said, her gaze moving over his face and then back to Raesha. "But she might not ever accept this baby."

He shook his head. "I can't leave one and take the other. They should be together."

"We will take care of Dinah until she is able," Naomi reminded him.

"And if she never can be able?" he asked, raking a hand down his face. "Does that mean I leave my niece here with you two and take my sister to be with family?"

"That is a question that you and Josie need to ask each other, I suppose," Naomi replied. "The child was left at our door. We won't turn her away."

"But I can be turned away. My sister and I?"

"She is not saying that," Raesha told him, her tone stern. "You are a grown man. You can go wherever you please. That baby doesn't have a choice."

So he went across the way, still wondering if Raesha loved Dinah and only tolerated him. If he had courage, he'd ask her outright. But he didn't think he was worthy of even that question.

Touching the door handle, he wondered what he'd do about Josie. He wouldn't leave her again. Maybe it would be better to leave the *bobbeli* and take his sister away from all the pain and memories.

Was that God's plan for him? For Raesha? For Josie?

Josiah said a prayer for patience and understanding and…for acceptance. He'd never been good at the acceptance part. He wanted to argue with the Lord and convince Him that Josiah knew best. But he knew nothing.

"I leave it in your hands, *Gott*."

No matter, he'd have to accept that in order to take care of his sister, he might have to leave Raesha and the child behind.

"I want to go home," Josie told him a few days later.

Surprised since she'd been venturing out to visit with Naomi on the porch, he studied his sister. The color was back in her face and she'd gained some weight back.

"Home? You mean to Ohio?"

She nodded. "That is the best place for us, don't you think? But we don't have to live with *Onkel*. I don't want to live with the family again."

Josiah felt the punch of a thousand fists inside his chest. So this was his answer, then?

"Why do you want to go back there?"

"I can't live here."

"What are you afraid of, sister?"

Josie stood and went to the kitchen window to stare across the way. "That house over there," she said.

So that was it. He'd have to sell the place and

move on, just as he'd planned. He'd never have a life with Raesha.

"And what about your child?"

"My child has found a home, Josiah. I am at peace with that."

Peace? She was at peace with that?

How could she be so cold, so detached?

Did that man do this to her? Take her soul?

He tried to think, tried to focus. "I still have to get the barn built. Men are coming in two days to do that."

"Don't rebuild the barn," she suggested.

"Why wouldn't I?" Josiah replied, tired and dejected.

Josie whirled to stare at him, her eyes bright with fear and anger. "Some things can't be rebuilt, Josiah."

And some things couldn't be forgiven, he decided. His sister would never forgive him for leaving her all those years ago.

"Josiah, I heard you're not rebuilding the barn," Raesha said the next day when he came to visit with Dinah.

He'd been quiet the last few days, in and out without eating or staying to visit. He hadn't gone to church last Sunday, citing he needed to stay with Josie.

People were beginning to take it for granted

that Dinah would grow up in the Bawell house. But they weren't so sure about Josiah and his sister. What was their story?

Raesha wanted to know the rest of that story, too.

She loved the man. She'd fought against it but now she could feel it each time he entered a room. That image of having him and Dinah with her didn't go away easily.

Now he gave her a glance that told her everything.

"You're leaving," she said, glad that they were alone. Naomi had taken Dinah out in the new stroller they'd found at the general store. Just for a brief walk along the drive.

He took her hand. "Josie wants to go back to Ohio."

"Does she, now?" Raesha tried to stifle the resentment she felt toward the girl. "I thought she didn't like it there."

"She likes it there better than here," he said. "I'm putting the place up for sale as is. I'll take any offers."

"And then you'll just go?"

"No. We leave next week. I've worked out the details through a real estate agency."

"I see." Angry that he hadn't explained any of this to her sooner, she nodded. "So just like that, you leave and go on with your life. Have either of you considered Dinah?"

"Yes. We want to leave her with you if you don't mind. You love her and she will be safe and happy here. I will send money to provide for her."

Pulling her hand away, Raesha asked, "So you will just walk away from her and me, Josiah?"

He looked up at her, his eyes as dark as a storm. "I have no other choice."

"Because Josie doesn't want her baby?"

"She is my sister and she has suffered enough."

"She might leave again."

"*Ja*, she might. But I have to do this. I wasn't here for her before and she has not forgotten that."

The pain tore through Raesha. The unfairness of it all crashed over her. She loved this man and she loved this baby.

But she had promised to accept what came. "How can I love Dinah without you here, Josiah?"

"You love her already," he said. "More than you will ever love me."

"You have no idea," she retorted, tears streaming down her face. "No idea at all about how much love I have to give."

"I want to stay," he said. "Raesha, I want to stay but I can't do it…and you can't leave."

"You never asked me."

"Because I know the answer. I heard you say it myself."

"You have a choice and you've made it. I understand." And because she was angry and hurt, she added, "You run away from the truth, Josiah. The truth that is right in front of your eyes."

He took her arm again, his eyes misty, his breath rising and falling with each word. "Do you think this is an easy choice? I want more than anything to be here with you and Dinah and take care of both of you. But Josie needs me."

Raesha was about to tell him to go, but a crash on the porch caused both of them to run to the back of the house.

Naomi lay on the porch floor, panting. "I'm sorry. She took Dinah. Josie took the child out of the stroller and ran away. I tripped over the steps. Had to alert you."

Raesha fell down beside Naomi and shouted at Josiah. "Go to the shop and call for a doctor. And then go and find you sister and Dinah."

She held her mother-in-law and prayed. For all of them.

Chapter Twenty

Josiah heard the siren coming up the road but he kept running, searching, calling out for his sister. He looked in the barn and the yard, around the closed shop. He peeked in windows and opened doors.

The stroller lay on its side in the driveway, just a few feet from the house. Why had his sister taken the baby she wanted no part of?

He kept searching. The whole community would be alerted soon and they'd help. Then they'd tell Josie she had to leave. He'd take her and go. He should have never returned to Campton Creek.

Running again. Raesha thought he was running but this time he was trying to do the right thing.

He looked over at the old place, the cold late afternoon dark with gloomy clouds making the house look broken and forlorn. Could she have gone there?

Hurrying across the arched bridge, he gulped in the chilly air and kept praying. *Why now, Josie? Why?*

Then he heard a baby crying inside the house.

"Josie?"

Josiah hurried up onto the porch and shook the door open. Then he followed the cries upstairs to the room that used to be Josie's.

And found her in a corner, holding Dinah tight, both of them crying.

"Josie," he said, sliding down on his knees. "Josie."

"I'm so sorry," she cried out. "I'm so sorry. I love her. I love my baby. But I can't take care of her."

"Why did you take her?" he asked, pushing at his sister's hair, checking to see that Dinah was all right.

"I heard you fighting with Raesha. She loves you and she loves Dinah. And I'm forcing you to leave both of them. I panicked. I thought if I took her away again, you could be with Raesha."

He sank down beside his sister and put an arm around her thin shoulders. "Why did you refuse to even look at the baby before?"

"I couldn't take it anymore," she admitted. "She reminded me of that night, that boy. I tried not to love her, brother. But I do."

The relief he felt swept through Josiah with a river-swift clarity. "I prayed that you would come to see that, Josephine. It will be okay. We will take Dinah with us and go home."

"No," Josie said. "*I* will go. Alone." Looking down at Dinah, she whispered, "But you need to stay. You belong here and so does she."

She handed him the baby and he cuddled Dinah close, his eyes on Josie. There had to be another reason she wanted to leave again. "Tell me what happened here, sister. Before I came back home."

Josie scooted toward the corner of the wall, sobbing. "I didn't mean to cause a fire, Josiah. I didn't."

"What?" Josiah calmed Dinah and then touched a hand to Josie's sweater. "What are you saying?"

"They were fighting. He…he hit Mamm. I was lighting lamps and I turned and ran to the barn, still holding a lamp." Gulping, she wiped at her eyes. "I was so scared I fell and dropped the lamp. It spilled onto a hay bale. The barn caught on fire."

Josiah closed his eyes, the horror of what had

happened cloaking him in darkness. "But you ran out? You didn't stay in the barn."

"I screamed and tried to get out," she said, her voice going calm now. "He came running and jerked me out of the way, threw me to the ground and told me I was stupid. He went inside."

Josiah could picture his angry father, pushing his child away, shouting his wrath. "Then what happened, Josie?"

"Mamm came running, her face all bruised. She went in after him, Josiah. She went in and I heard her scream. They never came out." Burying her face in her hands, Josie sobbed. "It was my fault. All my fault."

Josiah let out his own sob. All these years, his sister had carried a guilt far greater than anything he'd ever known. She believed she'd killed her parents.

"Josie, listen to me. This was not your fault, you hear me? This was an accident and not your fault."

His sister looked up at him, the little girl he remembered gone now. "But that's why God punished me. That's why I couldn't marry Tobias or take care of Dinah. *Gott* punished me and now I'll never be able to get married and have another child."

Josiah held his sobbing sister close and

wished he could take on her pain. "You are safe now. Gott loves you. He has brought you home, sister. And you are strong enough to tell the truth of all you've been through. Did you not know? He was there with you all along. For He has brought you home to heal."

"I don't believe that," Josie shouted. "I want to go away."

"Sister, listen to me," he said, seeing the path ahead in a new light. "We have both been running away from the truth. It's time we stop that. We don't have to live in this house but we have found a wonderful place where we can all live."

"You mean with Raesha and Naomi?" she asked, her voice cracking, her eyes full of uncertainty.

"They love us. They want us there. If you can't raise Dinah by yourself, they will gladly take on that task."

"They don't want *me* there."

"Yes, they do. They both do. Have you not seen what those two women have done for us?"

Wiping at her eyes, Josie bobbed her head. "*Ja*, I've seen it and felt it and cried because they have been so kind. But I'll be shunned and...no one will ever want me."

"*Gott* wants you," Josiah said, his hand rubbing Dinah's soft curls. "*Gott* wants us here."

"How can you be so sure?" she asked.

Josiah held Dinah close as he lifted up and reached out his hand to his sister. "Because here we are, back where we started, the truth between us clear. This is our opportunity to start over again with people who love us. That, sister, is *Gott*'s doing."

She shifted away, buried her face against her knees.

"Josie, we can stop running now."

Josie lifted her head and glanced around the empty room. "It's just a house, isn't it? A lonely old house."

"*Ja*, that is all—just wood and beams. But across that little bridge out there is a home. And it's waiting for us. Will you go there with me so I can tell Raesha how much I love her and want to marry her?"

Josie's smile started out small and then brightened to a big grin. "I never thought I'd hear you say such words."

"Neither did I," he admitted. "But no truer words have ever been said."

"And what if she refuses?"

"I'll keep hanging around until she sees the light."

Raesha sat by the bed, her hand gripping Naomi's. Her mother-in-law had finally dozed off to sleep. The doctor had deemed her fine and dandy after she'd insisted she had only a sore foot, bruised knee and some bruised pride.

"I made it to the porch but that crooked step got me," she kept saying. Followed by, "Have they found the children yet?"

"Not yet," Raesha had said fifteen minutes ago. Over an hour had passed and several people had gone off searching.

She did not know where Josiah, Josie and Dinah had gone.

Had he taken both of them away?

A knock at the front door caused her to drop Naomi's hand and stand up. Hurrying to the parlor, she closed the door to Naomi's room, then took a deep breath. Good news or bad? She didn't know how to pray.

When she opened the door, she found Ava Jane Weaver standing there. *"Kumm,"* she said, wondering if the woman would tell her the worst.

Ava Jane came inside and then turned toward Raesha. "They are all found," she said, her blue eyes full of understanding. "They will be home shortly."

Raesha sank down on the nearest chair. "I was so worried."

Ava Jane got her some water and then pulled up a kitchen chair to sit with her. "Jeremiah decided to check the house."

"You mean, Josiah's house?"

Ava Jane nodded. "He found them upstairs, talking. They were on their way back here but my *daed* and Jeremiah talked to Josiah about a lot of things."

"Will they have to leave?"

"I don't know but I hope not," Ava Jane said. "Jeremiah sent me to sit with you and Mammi Naomi."

"But you have the *kinder*."

"My sister is with them. She was staying over since we have baking to do early tomorrow. She helps me a lot these days."

"You have a *gut* sister."

The small talk calmed Raesha while her heart exploded with both despair and hope. What could they be discussing?

After a cup of tea and more talk, the door finally opened and Josiah walked in holding Dinah, his sister trailing behind him. Raesha glanced over at Ava Jane and then back to Josiah.

He looked frazzled but he also looked hopeful. Almost at peace. Then he looked at Ava Jane. "Your husband is waiting outside. *Denke* for staying with her."

"I'll go, then," Ava Jane said, getting up. She touched Raesha's arm. "If you need anything—"

"I appreciate you," Raesha said, hugging Ava Jane.

After her friend left, she stood near the kitchen table, her hand on a chair. "Are you all right?" she asked, her gaze moving over all of them.

Josiah brought Dinah to her, and leaned close. "We are better than all right."

Raesha took the baby onto her shoulder, her hand holding Dinah against her heart. The baby cooed and settled her head against Raesha's neck, the sweet smell of her bringing tears to Raesha's eyes.

Josie stepped forward. "I am sorry, Raesha, for taking Dinah. I thought if I took her back, you and Josiah could…make a life together. Without worrying about me."

Raesha's anger and fear disappeared. Josie looked as if she'd cried a flood of tears. "But you didn't do that."

"Neh," the girl said. "I went to the old place and prayed. Josiah found Dinah and me there."

"We had a long talk," he explained. "About a lot of things."

Raesha held steady, her backbone straightening, her head up. "So you're all going. Is that it, then?"

Josiah shook his head. *"Neh,* we are not going. That is, if you are willing to let us stay."

"But I thought—"

Josie came closer and touched her fingers to Dinah's unruly curls. "I can't raise her alone. I need my brother to help me."

"Of course you do," Raesha replied, her heart careening out of control. "I understand."

"*Neh*, you don't understand," Josiah said, smiling for the first time. "We need you with us."

"I can't go—"

"We want to stay," he said. "Raesha, will you listen and let me say what I need to say?"

"Well, get on with it, then."

Shaking his head, he took Dinah from her and passed her to Josie. The girl took the baby and smiled.

Raesha gripped the chair back so tightly, her knuckles were going stiff. She couldn't speak.

Josiah pried her hand from the chair and then took her other hand. "What I'm trying to say is that we want to stay here and... I want to marry you and raise Dinah with you."

Dizziness took over. She thought she might be floating on a cloud. "What?"

"He wants to marry you," Josie said. "And I talked with Mr. Troyer and his son-in-law and told them I want to stay here and I'm willing to confess all and be baptized. For life, Raesha. No more running. We want to call this our home."

"Yes, what she said," Josiah added, grinning from ear to ear. "Please, Raesha, will you say something?"

"She'd better say yes" came a steady voice from the other room. "Don't make me have to get up and come in there and talk some sense into all of you."

Raesha burst into laughter and then she burst into tears.

"I say yes," she told Josiah. "I say yes."

He pulled her into his arms and swung her around, laughing, crying, smiling. "I love you. I could never leave you."

Josie cried, too, soft, healing tears. "Can we stay, Raesha?"

"Yes," she said. "I want all of you here with me."

"I feel the same," Naomi called. "But will you please bring the celebration in here. I am missing out."

Josiah gave Raesha a quick kiss and then set her down. "Let's get in there before she hurts herself again."

He took Dinah back and then urged Raesha and Josie forward. Josie took Raesha's hand, her expression full of joy.

Together, they trooped into Naomi's room

and found her wide-awake and sitting up. "Tell me everything," she said. "I know the Lord had a hand in all of this and I need details."

Josiah and Josie sat down in chairs by the bed while Raesha sat in a rocking chair and held Dinah close. Then they explained what had happened when Josiah found Josie inside the old house.

"I'm so sorry," Josie kept saying.

"You are forgiven," Naomi replied. "And now, you two must forgive your father. You've paid the price of growing up in that house. Time for a new start, with us. We have so much to celebrate. Life, happiness and two of our own returning to the fold."

Dinah giggled and clapped her hands together.

"I agree," Naomi said, clapping her hands, too. "We've taken in many people in this old house, but you three have been the most challenging. And the most loved."

Josiah reached a hand out to Raesha. "I can't wait for the rest of the challenges. We are home at last."

Raesha's contentment turned into such joy she thought her heart would burst. "We are all home," she said, gratitude coloring her world.

A month later, Josiah Fisher married Raesha Bawell in a service held at the Bawell house.

Bishop King listened to them as they promised to love, cherish and care for each other through sickness and health, troubles and joy. Then the bishop held his hand over theirs and told them to go forth with the Lord's blessing and in his name.

Later, they hosted a barn raising across the way and a feast for the whole community, then sang hymns to celebrate their life together.

Raesha wore a new *kapp* stitched with delicate embroidery with one pink rose hidden in the stitches. For Dinah and for Mrs. Fisher. They would never forget.

Later, she and Josiah stood on the front porch, braced against the November chill.

"Thanksgiving is coming," he said, his arm around his wife's waist. "I am thankful for so many things."

"So am I," Raesha replied, her heart happy as she stared at the woven brown basket that now held pumpkins and mums, the basket that had brought her a child, a new family and more love than she could have ever imagined.

It would forever be her cornucopia, overflowing with blessings.

* * * * *

*Don't miss the previous book
in the Amish Seasons miniseries:*

Their Amish Reunion

*And be sure to check out Lenora Worth's
Men of Millbrook Lake miniseries:*

Lakeside Hero
Lakeside Sweetheart
Her Lakeside Family

Available now from Love Inspired!

Dear Reader,

What would you do if you found a baby on your porch? Widow Raesha Bawell didn't want to let go of the baby she found and soon circumstances kept her from having to give up sweet Dinah.

God sent her a baby but he also sent her a man who could become her second husband. Raesha had to show grace and strength while she wrestled with being true to God's will and holding on to her own heart. Josiah Fisher didn't want to stay in Campton Creek but... Raesha made him stand up and take notice. Together, they have to decide what is best for the baby and for his fragile sister, Josie.

But that's how life goes, no matter which community you live in. Things can change very quickly and either we turn to God for guidance and hope, or things turn to chaos. I hope you enjoyed this story. I have to admit, my emotions were all over the place by the time I finished it! But I did fall in love with these characters. They are now a part of Campton Creek. I hope you'll keep reading about this fascinating community that has become a part of my heart!

Until next time, may the angels watch over you. Always!

Lenora

Get 4 FREE REWARDS!

We'll send you 2 FREE Books
plus 2 FREE Mystery Gifts.

Love Inspired® Suspense books feature Christian characters facing challenges to their faith... and lives.

FREE Value Over **$20**

MUST ♥ DOGS COLLECTION

SAVE 30% AND GET A FREE GIFT!

Finding true love can be "ruff"— but not when adorable dogs help to play matchmaker in these inspiring romantic "tails."

YES! Please send me the first shipment of four books from the **Must ♥ Dogs Collection**. If I don't cancel, I will continue to receive four books a month for two additional months, and I will be billed at the same discount price of $18.20 U.S./$20.30 CAN., plus $1.99 for shipping and handling.* That's a 30% discount off the cover prices! Plus, I'll receive a FREE adorable, hand-painted dog figurine in every shipment (approx. retail value of $4.99)! I am under no obligation to purchase anything and I may cancel at any time by marking "cancel" on the shipping statement and returning the shipment. I may keep the FREE books no matter what I decide.

☐ 256 HCN 4331   ☐ 456 HCN 4331

Name (please print)

Address   Apt. #

City   State/Province   Zip/Postal Code

> **Mail to the Reader Service:**
> **IN U.S.A.:** P.O. Box 1867, Buffalo, NY. 14240-1867
> **IN CANADA:** P.O. Box 609, Fort Erie, Ontario L2A 5X3

PETSBPA19

READERSERVICE.COM

Manage your account online!

- Review your order history
- Manage your payments
- Update your address

> ### *We've designed the Reader Service website just for you.*

Enjoy all the features!

- Discover new series available to you, and read excerpts from any series.
- Respond to mailings and special monthly offers.
- Browse the Bonus Bucks catalog and online-only exculsives.
- Share your feedback.

Visit us at:
ReaderService.com

RS16R